# THE ANGEL PROPHECY

## BOOK FIVE OF THE HUNTER FILES

### ROB JONES

Boldwood

First published in Great Britain in 2025 by Boldwood Books Ltd.

Cover Design by Tom Sanderson

Cover Images: Colin Thomas and Shutterstock

A CIP catalogue record for this book is available from the British Library.

Paperback ISBN 978-1-80600-037-1

Large Print ISBN 978-1-80600-036-4

Hardback ISBN 978-1-80600-035-7

Trade Paperback ISBN 978-1-80635-345-3

Ebook ISBN 978-1-80600-038-8

Kindle ISBN 978-1-80600-039-5

Audio CD ISBN 978-1-80600-030-2

MP3 CD ISBN 978-1-80600-031-9

Digital audio download ISBN 978-1-80600-034-0

This book is printed on certified sustainable paper. Boldwood Books is dedicated to putting sustainability at the heart of our business. For more information please visit https://www.boldwoodbooks.com/about-us/sustainability/

Boldwood Books Ltd, 23 Bowerdean Street, London, SW6 3TN

www.boldwoodbooks.com

*For my children*

# 1

Aleksey Petkevich walked briskly through the narthex of his local church and into the nave. It was dimly lit by a few simple religious candles, and apart from himself, empty. The priest was nowhere to be seen, just as Petkevich had ordered. He wanted this place to himself and the priest had no choice but to obey. Petkevich wore a plain but expensive black suit, a neatly laundered and pressed black shirt and an expensive black silk tie. As he walked down the central aisle of the nave, his leather loafers slapped pleasingly on the floor, echoing throughout the entire ancient building. Finally reaching the altar, he made a solemn sign of the cross in front of himself and then knelt in submission to his God.

He now reached into his suit pocket and pulled out a simple prayer rope. It had been handed down to him by his father who had received it from *his* father and so it went all the way up the line. Its thirty-three knots symbolised the thirty-three years Jesus Christ spent on Earth before ascending to Heaven, and now Petkevich gently rubbed the rope in his hand and began to pray.

'Господи, змилуйся надо мною.'

*Lord, have mercy on me.*

As was his custom, he repeated it twelve times, the words drifting from his dry lips like smoke. His utterance hummed gently in the enormous Eastern Orthodox Church, one of the largest in all of Belarus. He had spent much time here, but more so when he was younger. These days he had little spare time, but his generous donations to the church went some small way to relieving the guilt. His money had helped repair the roof and restore the beautiful sanctuary to its former glory, including the Holy Doors and a seven-hundred-year-old Christ Pantokrator, a stunning depiction of Christ made by dazzling golden mosaic tiles. Perhaps the Lord would have mercy on him after all, but it would be a close-run thing considering how he had spent much of his life.

He grew silent and turned his mind's attention inwards to the suffering and torment he had visited upon so many others. But he always had God in his heart. He never hurt anyone who wasn't a sinner. And this world was a world of sin, God knew that as well as he did. When he looked around him he saw nothing but sin. When he walked through the streets of his hometown, he saw nothing but debauchery and filth. When he looked elsewhere in the West, he saw the most degenerate and disgusting places that had ever existed in the long and tortured history of the world. It was a culture overspilling with every imaginable kind of violent, disgusting perversions. It made him feel sick just to think about it. But worse than any of that, Westerners were not content with turning their own world into a violent, wretched Sodom. They were intent on exporting their filth to the rest of the world. In the opinion of Aleksey Petkevich, what had for so long been called the West – a supposed beacon of light to those tortured souls living behind the Iron Curtain long ago – was now a crumbling, failed experiment filled with unhappy and broken people whose very souls had been utterly corrupted by wickedness and depravity that was to be found everywhere in their world. That was what they wanted for his world too. But he would never let that happen.

Petkevich was a thinking man, and a thinking man always had a plan. Petkevich's plan was ambitious – he knew that better than anyone. It involved tens of thousands of hours of research collected from some of the most ancient churches and libraries to be found anywhere in Europe. It involved an endless, diligent sifting through the sands of history in search of a dark and primeval truth that he intended to bring to the world. It involved an unshakeable faith in his most sacred belief that he was in this world to bring light to darkness and order to chaos.

It involved the most ancient, powerful and glorious prophecy ever made, a prophecy that if fulfilled, would make him as mighty as God.

Over the past few years, he had interviewed religious men who had spent decades toiling in the service of their God; he had collected countless objects of antiquity, always with specific religious provenances that would help him in his quest to fulfil this ancient prophecy, defeat evil and bring light back to a broken and immoral world. But there was one thing that still eluded him. There was one ancient object – some would call it a relic, but they would be wrong – that he needed more than any of these other things if he was to defeat evil and bring salvation to the people of the world.

The sword of the Archangel Michael.

And he knew who had it.

He had spoken with those people, those who had stolen the sacred sword – he believed they called themselves the HARPA team. They were led by an obnoxious, cocky archaeologist from England called Dr Maximillian Hunter. Then there was Agent Amy Fox – Amy was short for Amadea; he had learned this from minions working beneath him in his mighty empire. She was a former FBI agent who had transferred to HARPA, a subsidiary division of the FBI, some years ago, although her new role still allowed her to carry and use the FBI badge. Then there was Salvatore Blanco, a former all-round tough guy – soldier, helicopter pilot, a man who had even dabbled in some professional wrestling – a man who, from what he could tell, wanted nothing more than an early, much overdue retirement making pizzas. Next up was a young woman called Jodie Priest – she was the feisty one, the one with the fighting chops. Fast driver, too. She didn't scare him any more than any of the others. The truth was, the only one who scared him was called Quinn Mosley. She would scare anyone who knew what she was capable of but, luckily for him, she was now his prisoner. As were the Director of HARPA Jim Gates and his wife Susanna, and the director of UNESCO – Max Hunter's former boss – Dr Juliette Bonnaire. All four of them were now being held against their will in a secure location, somewhere no one would ever find them.

Now if the Good Lord permitted, Petkevich would be allowed to conduct a simple business transaction. Hunter and the rest of the HARPA team – sans Quinn Mosley, of course – would hand him the Sword of the Archangel Michael, which they had stolen, and in return, he would let their teammates live. But this was a lie. He had no intention of letting their teammates live, nor Hunter or anyone else in HARPA, because he never let any of his enemies or opponents live. If he won the game, he won their lives.

He had already made this proposal to Amy Fox when he had called her while she was in a hotel in Cornwall. She did not yet know who he really was because Aleksey Petkevich liked to play inside the shadows. He had called himself Oriax, and those mercenaries who worked for him were his Illuminated Ones. Some thought of them as demons, but that was not right. He was a man of God, in his own way. He wanted the Sword of the Archangel Michael because Michael had used it to drive Lucifer from Heaven, and now he wanted it to cleanse the West in his own image. He dreamt of wielding the powerful sword and saw himself surrounded by bright white light as he did God's work. Some said he was insane, but this was wrong too. He was a visionary and would bring great healing to the world. Just as soon as he had harnessed God's power and driven all the filth into the seas.

That was the dream of Aleksey Petkevich, and he intended to make it real.

## 2

Max Hunter looked out across Tintagel Haven at Merlin's Castle and stared at the ancient coast in the cold, early morning sunrise. A crisp south-westerly gust buffeted him, bringing the salted air of the Atlantic onto the land all around him. He was unsure immediately what he should do. He was aware of the others back inside the hotel, waiting for him to make a decision, and this time it was entirely down to him. Just moments ago Amy had asked him what he thought they should do, but the problem was he didn't know.

A man who called himself Oriax had just made a menacing telephone call to Amy and issued some terrible threats to the team relating to their current mission. He had told them that he had kidnapped their teammate Quinn Mosley, as well as their boss Jim Gates and his wife Susanna, and also Hunter's former boss at UNESCO, Professor Juliette Bonnaire. He had made threats against their lives unless they returned the Sword of the Archangel Michael, which HARPA had found at Merlin's Castle the previous evening. Oriax had described a simple trade – they give him the sword and he would give them their friends. If they did not give him the sword, he would kill their friends.

Not only that, but Ben Lewis's wife, Meg, had called in the night and told the former US Marine that his son was in the ICU after having been taken gravely ill with pneumonia. Doctors were concerned about his condition, and after a brief consultation with the team, Lewis had fled the hotel in the night in a local cab. He had not been in touch since leaving, but Hunter knew by now he was probably on one of the first flights back to the States.

Hunter had much to consider. First, Oriax was clearly a maniac and his word could not be trusted. There was no reason to believe that should they give him the sword, he would keep his promise and return their friends. He thought grimly there was no evidence that any of their friends were still alive, but he doubted this was true. Oriax would want to keep his hostages alive as long as possible and use them to barter. He had already made his first demands based on the value of their lives and there could be more to come. The second thing Hunter had to consider was the ethical repercussions of giving a man like Oriax the sword. They had only found this magnificent relic a few hours ago, and there was simply no way yet to understand its powers. They could prove to be truly breathtaking, dangerous even, especially in the wrong hands. He knew that if ever there was a case of there being 'the wrong hands', then these hands surely belonged to Oriax.

Hunter saw something out of the corner of his eye and turned to see Amy. She had left the company of the others back in the warmth of the hotel and strolled out to him to where he stood now on the cliff edge, looking across the peninsula at the ancient ruins of Merlin's Castle.

'How's it going?' Amy asked.

Hunter shrugged boyishly. He was one of the world's most

accomplished and respected archaeologists, not only with degrees of distinction from some of the best universities on earth but also many years of fieldwork behind him in which he had built a strong reputation for producing quality material in strong academic papers. More recently, he had been forced to use this knowledge alongside his earlier experience as an officer in the Grenadier Guards in the British Army, while working for HARPA – the Heritage, Artifacts, and Relics Protection Agency. This was a US government agency based out of Washington DC. He had worked alongside Agent Amy Fox, formerly of the FBI; Sal Blanco, a former American Army pilot and pizza chef-in-waiting; Jodie Priest, a dropout runaway cat burglar from California whose favourite pastime was breaking into expensive high-powered cars and taking them for joyrides; Ben Lewis, a former Marine and theological scholar; and finally Quinn Mosley, a young computer hacker about whom no one knew the first thing, except her loyalty and humour. Despite all of this, though, Max Hunter could still easily revert to a state of almost childish silliness. His humour was sarcastic and cynical and altogether too British, especially for Amy Fox.

'What does that shrug mean?' she asked.

'The truth is, I don't know how it's going, but I know one thing – we can't give those bastards the sword.'

'I know that,' Amy said. She pulled her collar up around her neck, buttoned her jacket and thrust her hands in her pockets, shivering. 'Damn, this is a cold wind.'

'You're used to much colder in New England,' Hunter said, alluding to Amy's upbringing in Boston.

'And Washington DC too, for that matter,' Amy said. 'But there's something different about this wind.'

'Must be the sea,' Hunter said. 'I'm a proper landlubber, so I wouldn't know. England never really gets that cold in the winter. It's more of an endless damp, grey gloom. Enjoy.'

'Max, you're rambling.'

He nodded in agreement. 'I know I am. It's because I don't know what to do. Normally our orders come down from the US government via Jim, but now he's, well, not available... we're working entirely on our own. You're Jim's second-in-command, but I don't want to push all of this onto you. You just asked me what we should do and the answer is I don't know, but I don't want to give them the sword under any circumstances. We don't know what it's capable of and we don't know what Oriax is capable of either. It would just be incredibly irresponsible of us to hand over an ancient biblical weapon of unknown power to a man like that.'

The wind was playing havoc with Amy's hair, and now she swept some of it back and attempted to tuck it behind her ear. It didn't work. 'Of course it would, and I'm not saying that we should do that. But I think we need to play things smart for a little while because there's no way I am going to let Quinn, Jim, Susanna or Professor Bonnaire die.'

Hunter stared down at his boots and aimlessly kicked at some turf. 'I know, I agree. I'm not going to let that happen either. So we need to move fast before this gets out of control. If there's one thing I've learnt on all of these missions we've had together, it's that we cannot let things get ahead of us. We have to be in control of this and that means we always stay one step ahead of the enemy.'

'Agreed,' Amy said.

Hunter paused a beat. 'How are Sal and Jodie?'

'They're good. Last time I checked they were having a cup of coffee over in the dining room. They're serving breakfast in there but neither of them felt like eating.'

'I can understand that, but we do need to eat. I don't know what we're going to decide to do, but whatever it is, it's going to happen fast so we're going to need all of the sustenance we can get before we go and get our friends back – which I think we can do.'

'You have an idea now then?'

'I think so. It's not much of one but I think it's our only play. C'mon – let's go and join Sal and Jodie in the dining room and grab some breakfast. I'll tell you what I'm thinking about.'

# 3

After spending so long out on the clifftop, Hunter was grateful to get back inside the friendly warmth the hotel dining room. He had travelled all over the world and there seemed to be something uniquely pleasant about a British seaside hotel. He wasn't quite sure what that was, and he certainly had no time to think about it now – all he knew was that it was of some small comfort during this terrible time to find himself sitting at the dining table in front of a large bay window, looking out across the coast, with a hot, steaming cup of tea and a pile of freshly buttered toast in front of him.

'So what's our game plan?' Blanco asked.

'Oriax told us we were to wait for further instructions and I think that when he calls us, our game plan should be to do exactly what he demands,' Hunter said. 'We tell him we agree to the trade. We tell him we'll meet him at the place and time of his choosing. Let him think he's entirely in control.'

'Are you crazy?' Jodie asked. 'We can't give that total asshole the sword! We don't even know what it can do yet!'

'No, I am not crazy,' Hunter said, 'because we're not actually going to give him the sword. The key part of the plan is that we're going to tell them he can have it to keep him happy, but we're not just going to sit around and wait for the deadline. We're going to get busy.'

'Okay,' Blanco said. 'I'm following you so far, but busy how??'

'We hunt them down,' Hunter said grimly. 'We use absolutely everything at our disposal to find out exactly who this Oriax is and where he is based. Then we get to him before the deadline to trade the sword, rescue our friends and keep the sword safe.'

'That's it?' Jodie said. She finished her coffee and slid down in her seat. 'That's your entire plan? Your plan is that we are going to track down and beat up the baddies?'

'No, my plan is that we appear to them completely beaten and terrified that Oriax is going to kill our team. We accept his demands; we let him think that he's holding all the cards and that we value the lives of our friends over the sword. We play the sword's powers down, psychologically manipulating him into thinking that we don't know what we've got on our hands. We'll make him believe we're prepared to make the trade. Then we'll get to him through some kind of back channel and rescue Quinn and the others, long before the deadline.'

'I don't know,' Amy said. 'That sounds kind of risky, Max.'

'Of course it's risky! Everything in life is risky, Amy. Especially what we do in HARPA. There's just no way that we can get through this without taking that risk, and the lives of Quinn and our friends are worth any risk, in my humble opinion.'

Blanco's face grew serious. 'You're damn right they are.'

'Humble,' Jodie said. 'Pfft.'

Hunter watched Blanco's hand move across the table and squeeze Jodie's hand. They had a unique relationship, almost like the bond found between father and daughter, and Hunter realised what this little hand squeeze meant – that although he would never say it out loud, Blanco was glad that they hadn't snatched Jodie. He wouldn't say it out loud because he was too much of a decent guy for people to think he was glad they had taken Quinn instead, but that is what Hunter thought his old friend was thinking.

'Okay,' Amy said. 'Whatever we think of it, it's the only plan we've got. For what it's worth, I think we should give it a shot. The only problem could be he might not give us much of a deadline.'

'We'll work with whatever he gives us and if it's not long enough, we'll try and stall for time,' Hunter said.

Amy nodded. 'Okay. There's not a lot else we can do anyway except just give in to their demands completely and hand over the sword. And none of us is going to do that. I'm happy to go along with trying to deceive them, but what I don't get is how the hell we're going to find out where they're keeping Quinn and the others in the meantime.'

'Yeah, that's what I was thinking,' Blanco said. 'Normally we would get Quinn onto that part of the problem and she'd get her computer out and start tapping away and the next thing you'd know, we'd know exactly where we need to go. As I'm sure we all realise, none of us has her skills though so I think that leaves us up shit creek without a paddle.'

'That's not entirely true,' Hunter said, turning to Amy. 'You're a highly respected former FBI agent. I know the remit of the Bureau is within the United States, but you must have contacts or be able to do something with that telephone call you just had with Oriax. Remember, Jim Gates is a senior member of the US government working in the intelligence agencies. You get on the phone to whoever you can think of and see if you can get some help tracing that call... or any other information you can get about it. Use Jim's name to open doors.'

Amy was already on her feet, pulling her phone from her

pocket. She walked across the room and began pacing up and down the far end of the dining room, which was mostly empty of guests. Hunter, Blanco and Jodie exchanged a few nervous glances of anticipation as they waited for her to come back over, which she did after fifteen minutes that felt like forever. In Hunter's opinion, this was a good thing because it meant she might have got somewhere.

'Please tell us you've caught some kind of a break?' Jodie asked.

'Maybe,' Amy said, 'but it's vague. I was able to use a mutual friend of mine and Jim's who works in the CIA's intelligence electronic signals surveillance department. He worked some magic on my cell phone data and told me that the call was made from a location in London.'

'You think Oriax is in London?' Blanco asked.

'I have no idea where he is,' Amy said. 'I don't even know who the man is, so as far as I'm concerned he could be literally anywhere in the world. All I know is that the call to my phone was made from a specific location in London.'

Hunter finished his tea. 'It looks like we've got the first step on our journey sorted out then.'

Jodie looked around. 'What's the quickest way out of here?'

'Through the door,' Hunter said.

'I meant Cornwall.'

'The quickest way out of here,' Hunter continued, 'is not very quick at all. We're at the very end of England and there aren't even any motorways here. Our best bet would be to get to Exeter as quickly as possible and from there take a train to London.'

'Exactly how long is that going to take?' Amy asked. 'Wouldn't it be quicker to fly from Exeter to London?'

'No, I don't think so,' Hunter said. 'That can turn into a bit of a nightmare and by the time you've messed around at airports on either side of the flight, it can take nearly as long. It's almost half past six now. It'll be one hour to Exeter by car and then there's a train leaving Exeter St. Davids at seven fifty-two that gets us into London just before ten. We can make it if we get moving right now.'

'I agree,' Amy said. 'So let's get going!'

**4**

As the train made its way northeast through England, Hunter closed his eyes and tuned out from the hubbub of the carriage to focus on their current predicament. It was clear that thanks to his hard work over the last few days, Oriax had a distinct advantage over the HARPA team. They would all have to raise their game and fight harder than ever before if they were to achieve their twin goals of rescuing their teammates and keeping the sword of the Archangel Michael out of their enemy's hands.

And that was no easy thing to achieve.

Looking over the past few years of service with HARPA, he was reminded of some of the maniacs they had gone up against in order to protect the world, in some cases from unimaginable levels of catastrophic violence. His thoughts drifted lazily from one mission to the next – visions of fighting in Greenlandic ice caves to storming fortresses in Slovenia and then back again to landing in Switzerland to meet Oscar Rorschach for the first time. As his team chatted quietly around him, he was sucked once more down memory lane to the time they had watched Olaf Skulberg raise the *Titanic* in the North Atlantic, and the moment he would never forget as he watched the majestic bow section rising up on Skulberg's ingenious AI nanopillow.

It had been a wild ride and hopefully there was a lot more to come, but as he opened his eyes and watched the English countryside race by in a blur, his attention was soon captivated by Amy and an update to her earlier briefing. While he had been daydreaming, she had received another message from her contact in the CIA back in Washington DC.

'That was George calling again,' she said.

'He has a name now?' Jodie said.

Amy nodded. 'Sure. George Pak. He's been analysing the phone call made to my cell phone this morning in a little more detail, and he's certain of the location in London, but he also believes there's a strong chance that some sort of spoofing software was used.'

Jodie was chewing a sandwich she had bought at the station. 'You mean we're on a wild goose chase?'

'Possibly,' Amy said, 'but I don't think so. George thinks that Oriax made the telephone call from a secure location somewhere else and bounced it through the London site to produce a fake location just in case it was traced.'

'I'd expect nothing less,' Blanco said.

'Me too,' Hunter said. 'I don't want that rotten bastard to make anything too easy for us because I really want to enjoy it when we win.'

Amy said, 'Like I say, he likely used spoofing software and so George says that we're probably not going to find Oriax at the location, but I think that we're probably going to find something that can lead us to him.'

'It still all sounds so tenuous,' Blanco said. 'I feel we've rarely worked with less.'

Amy looked at him, her eyes imploring him to be more

supportive. 'Sal, it's all we've got. They've taken Quinn and the others and we've done the best we can do by contacting George and asking him to trace the call. And he's done his best by telling us that it was sent via a spoof caller ID positioned in London. I can still draw on crimefighting experience in the FBI here. I think that Oriax will have a criminal network surrounding him, and he will have farmed out the order to spoof the call and someone in his organisation would have put it through somewhere that they know. But I'm certain it's some kind of property connected to Oriax in some way.'

'That is one hell of a stretch,' Jodie said.

'It is one hell of a stretch,' Hunter agreed. 'But as Amy has just said, we really have no other choice other than to follow this lead.'

'But we're still not giving up the damned sword, are we?' Jodie asked.

As she spoke, Jodie looked at the large backpack now in between Blanco's legs, rocking gently backwards and forwards with the motion of the train. Inside were some of their spare clothes and personal effects and, it just so happened, the Sword of the Archangel Michael.

'No, we're definitely not going to give them the sword,' Hunter said. 'Remember, when Oriax calls to give us his new instructions, we're going to accept his demands – or at least that's what we're going to tell him. Then if the deadline for the trade is too close, we're going to ask for more time and we'll see what he says. We'll see what kind of offer he makes in terms of where he wants to trade the sword. We'll just have to take it from there.'

'So much of this is making me deeply unhappy,' Jodie said.

Hunter leaned forward and gave her a reassuring look. 'Jodie, this is not like one of our normal missions. In the past, we've always found ourselves at the beginning of a clue trail leading to some kind of ancient treasure. The first time we ever worked together we found Atlantis. The second time we found the Revelation Relic. Then we helped to raise the *Titanic*! After that, we found this...' As he spoke, he nodded his head subtly to Blanco's backpack. 'The Sword of Archangel Michael. This mission is very different from the others. This time, one of our team members and several other people who are very important to us have been snatched and we don't know where they are. We're not being asked to find some ancient treasure, we're being asked to rescue our friends and bring our team back together. But we have to tackle it the same way we always do. If we can put our heads together as we have done in the past, we can make this work.'

Jodie nodded, at least temporarily satisfied by Hunter's explanation. Like the rest of the team, she understood implicitly that this mission was very different from the others, and Hunter could tell from the look on her face that she was unhappy about that. Insofar as they were any kind of team at all, the HARPA team had trained and cut their teeth specifically on the discovery of ancient sites and the retrieval of ancient treasures. Now they were being asked to give one of those treasures to a very unsavoury individual in return for the lives of their friends. The truth was, Hunter thought with a little surprise, that this was without a doubt one of the most important missions the team had ever done together. This time, failure meant the deaths of Quinn Mosley, Jim and Susanna Gates and Professor Juliette Bonnaire, and there would be no one to blame but themselves.

Hunter stood up from his seat and strolled along the corridor to take a look through another further along. He was pleased to see that they had passed Reading and were racing eastwards towards London. The final destination of the train was Paddington, where they intended to get out and take a taxi to the location George Pak had found when working on Amy's phone – a small side street in Camden. Hunter knew the area, not well but enough. As a student, he had spent a lot of time in North London, including Camden, where he'd watched some bands in the pub near the bridge. It was a quirky and slightly bohemian part of the city that he used to enjoy very much, but he had not been to Camden Town for nearly thirty years. That in itself promised to be an exciting experience, of which he had no doubt.

The train finally reached its destination at Paddington, and Hunter and the team were glad to be able to disembark and stretch their legs along the platform in the world-famous station. At that very moment, Amy's phone began to ring. It was Oriax.

'What do I do?' Amy asked, uncharacteristically uncertain.

'Speak to the bastard,' Jodie said. 'And remember to stall for time.'

Amy put the phone to her ear to answer the call. 'This is Special Agent Amy Fox.'

'You're getting all formal with me, Amy,' Oriax said. 'And here I was thinking that we were getting so much closer.'

'What do you want, you creep?'

'Tut, tut, tut! I don't think it's very wise to be insulting a man who is holding so many of your precious friends captive! Would you agree with me that calling me a creep was a very silly and dangerous thing to do?'

Amy calmed herself down. 'What do you want, Oriax?'

'Ah! I see Special Agent Amy Fox is not only formal but also keen to get down to business. This is good. This is also how I feel because I too want to get down to business. You will recall that in our last telephone call, I told you that you would be sent further instructions in good time and that you were not to do anything stupid in the meantime. I do hope that you paid good attention to me and followed my advice?'

'What are your further instructions?'

'My further instructions are that you are to bring the Sword of the Archangel Michael to Cairo and I expect you to be there within forty-eight hours. You will meet me at the Giza Necropolis, specifically on the east side of the Pyramid of Khafre at midday tomorrow, local time. I will be there with your friends, colleagues and associates who will be handed over to you in perfectly good health, should you be able to deliver the Sword of Archangel Michael to me and my team. Once we have verified that it is the authentic sword and that it is undamaged, your friends will be returned to you and then you may all go on to lead your lives with my blessing.'

'Yeah, right,' Amy said. 'Just how the hell can we be expected to trust a man like you? You've already kidnapped four completely innocent people.'

'No one is ever completely innocent. And you cannot be expected to trust me. You must simply put your faith in God.'

'That's not a very compelling argument coming from a man like you.'

Oriax's tone changed, his voice now growing colder and strangely calmer. 'You do not know the first thing about me, Amy Fox! You cannot judge my character and you cannot see my soul!'

'We'll be at the pyramid's east side at noon, Oriax,' Amy said. 'And you'd better bring our friends. If they're harmed in any way, I will bring hellfire down on you, so help me God!'

Oriax laughed. 'And yet I will be the one holding the Sword of the Archangel Michael! One wonders how that hellfire threat might work out in such circumstances. Just do as I say, Amy Fox... and don't do anything stupid or you can absolutely count on your friends getting killed.'

Amy was about to respond when the line was cut dead.

She turned to Hunter and the rest of the team, all of whom

had been listening to the call on speakerphone. 'What the hell did you make of that?'

'That Oriax needs the careful attention of a mental health specialist as soon as possible,' Hunter said.

Blanco huffed out a laugh. 'At least we didn't have to ask for more time.'

'Sal's right,' Hunter said. 'Two days is more than enough time for us to work our magic.'

Amy frowned. 'Two days seems like a very long time for a deadline to me. I wonder why?'

'He must have his reasons,' Jodie said.

'I just hope we can save the others before the deadline,' Blanco said. 'I really don't want to go to Cairo and hand the sword over to a man like Oriax.'

Amy looked at the backpack he was carrying, containing the sword. 'We might have to do it if we can't get to Quinn and the others before the deadline.'

'And all we have is some crappy information about the phone call being spoofed through a location in Camden,' Jodie said. 'It feels like we're playing with Quinn's life, and the lives of all the others!'

'We're not playing with anyone's lives,' Hunter said. 'Everybody, just calm down. Stick to the plan. This is exactly what we wanted to hear from Oriax! He has given us enough time for us to be able to track him down and get to him before the deadline. If we can strike before that, he won't be expecting us. We'll have the element of surprise on our side.'

'If,' Jodie said with emphasis, '*if* we can find them before the deadline. What happens if we go off on some wild goose chase and end up in goddamn Japan and can't get to Cairo by the deadline?'

'Oh ye of little faith,' Hunter said, turning to Amy. 'Can you call George Pak and get him to run this number the way he did the last one?'

'Sure,' Amy said. 'I'll do it straight away.'

Hunter watched Amy walk the length of the platform and back again and by the time she returned to them, she had the information they wanted to hear. 'Same place. George says the call was made from the location in Camden.'

'Well, isn't life full of happy coincidences?' Hunter said. 'Because we're going to be there in less than half an hour. Hopefully, that will be the first stepping stone to finding Oriax before his deadline down in Cairo.'

'Hopefully,' Jodie said. 'But hope is pretty hard to come by these days.'

# 5

Approaching quarter past ten, Hunter gazed out of the window of the Black Cab they had hailed outside Paddington Station. They were driving up the High Street on their way to Camden Lock. He was pleasantly surprised to see that far from the image in his mind of a decayed town, in thirty years worse repair, it actually looked nicer than his last visit. He'd read something about that in a newspaper – apparently they called it 'gentrification'. Hunter wasn't entirely sure what that meant but understood it meant locals could no longer afford to buy a cup of coffee here. Either way, it was a pleasant drive along a neat street lined with fashionable clothes stores, art supplies shops and the obligatory series of coffee shops. They passed under the famous railway bridge and Hunter was pleased to see the large green rectangle painted on the side, filled with the words 'Camden Lock' in bright yellow paint, still there after all these years.

'I used to drink down there,' Hunter said to Jodie, pointing up Castlehaven Road. 'There was a great little place up there called The Red Lion. Man, I could tell you some stories about that place!'

'Yeah, don't bother,' Jodie said. 'If there's one thing I don't need in my life right now, it's some old English dude telling me all about how great everything was thirty years ago.'

'I was going to make no such case,' Hunter said. 'But mostly it was, now you come to mention it. Too bad you weren't even born then, so you'll never know.'

They turned left at Camden Lock Bridge and made their way down Paddock Lane, passing more pubs and nightclubs that at night would be busy venues bustling with cashed-up clients, but were quiet and strangely lifeless in the daytime. Eventually, they found themselves at the address George Pak had given Amy back in Cornwall – an expensively refurbished warehouse, made of beautiful yellow polychrome bricks and with black arched windows. Amy asked the cabbie to pull over and after they had got out of the car, she asked him to wait.

'The very height of gentrification,' Hunter said to himself. 'I guess.'

'Well, this is the place,' Amy said. 'This is where George said both phone calls from Oriax originated from.'

'Maybe we might get lucky,' Jodie said as it began to rain. She looked up at the sky and cursed, and then pulled her collar up. 'I mean, maybe we'll actually find Oriax here, after all.'

'Something tells me it's not going to be that easy, Jodie,' Blanco said. 'I don't think anything we've ever done has been that straightforward.'

'I agree with Sal,' Amy said. 'This Oriax guy is not going to be a pushover. Don't forget, he already managed to kidnap Quinn and the others. He's a man with resources. He has a strategic mind and a ruthless streak, which he thinks he can exploit to get the sword from us.'

'He thinks he can,' Hunter said. 'But I think he's got another thing coming.'

'Maybe,' Blanco said. 'But I'm not counting any chickens yet.'

The team reached a black-painted door at the front of the converted warehouse and saw a small panel to the right of the door containing six surnames with adjacent buzzers.

'Logan, Chandra, Taylor, White, Collins or Kwakye?' Blanco asked.

'Oh, it's like a lucky dip!' Jodie said. 'Which one of these guys is working for an international psychopath whose hobby is collecting dangerous weapons from the Bible? Anyone want to guess which one?'

Hunter gave her a look and shook his head. 'Amy, is there no way your friend in Georgetown can narrow this down at all?'

'That's not the way it works, Max,' she said. 'George got a GPS signal which has given us this location; unfortunately, he can't tell us which apartment inside this warehouse was actually the specific location for the phone call.'

Hunter lifted his collar against the weather. The wind was cutting across at a vertical angle that was blowing rain right down inside his jacket. He shuffled closer to the warehouse wall in a bid to stay a little drier and had another think about the surnames. Even though he had frowned at her comment, Jodie had not been far wrong when she had described the situation as a lucky dip. Luckily, at that moment, they saw somebody shuffling down the stairs at the rear of the lobby through the window. An elderly woman who now opened the door smiled at them and disappeared off into the bustling crowd, walking along the pavement. Amy had read Hunter's mind, because before he said anything, she stuck her foot out and stopped the door from closing.

'Shall we?' she said, gesturing her hand in a sweeping motion into the lobby.

'I thought you'd never ask,' Hunter said, looking up at the rain and the grizzly grey sky producing it. 'Maybe when we find this place, whoever's working with Oriax might offer us a nice cup of tea and a biscuit?'

'Let's just see if we can find him first,' Amy said.

'Yeah, get out of my way, Hunter. I'm soaking wet,' Jodie said, pushing past him and stepping into the lobby. She shook the rain from her coat and hair and walked over to the first door. Everyone joined her inside the lobby and Blanco gently closed the door behind him.

'Are you just going to knock on the first door?' Hunter asked Jodie.

'Yeah. Don't forget I'm a thief, Hunter. We knock first and if someone answers then we read off a script. If they don't answer, I use my little magical skills to break into their house and then we search the place.'

Hunter stared at her. 'Search for what? A secret diary detailing all of Oriax's evil plans?'

'Listen, weren't you the one back on the train telling me we just have to work with what we have?'

Hunter apologised. 'I'm sorry. I didn't mean to be sarcastic.'

Jodie knocked on the door, and a moment later, an elderly man answered it and asked them what they wanted.

Hunter stepped to the door and looked past the old man into the apartment as he was talking to Jodie. It was a normal residential apartment, and he could see the hall down to the kitchen where steam bubbled up from a pan. He could smell fried vegetables in the air and maybe some roast chicken too. He could also hear the sound of talk radio blathering away in the background.

Tugging Jodie's elbow, she turned to look at him and then stepped back.

Hunter stepped up to the man and asked him if he had any problems with his neighbours.

'Who are you people?' the old man asked, looking at them
suspiciously.

'We're with the council,' Amy said, quickly flashing her FBI
badge at the man. He looked at it for a moment, confused, and
then shrugged and looked Amy in the eye.

'What is the council doing here?'

'We've had several complaints about a noisy neighbour in the
apartment block and we're just trying to make sure there's no
problem. We just want to have a friendly word with him.'

Hunter turned and rolled his eyes, but was amazed when the
man gave Amy a useful answer.

'Then try on the top floor,' the old man said, half-closing the
door on them. 'They're terrible up there. Luckily I'm right the way
down here so they're not too much of a problem for me, but some
of the other neighbours have been driven crazy by it. They're
always coming and going, in and out. Young people. They look
like trouble to me. One of them looked at me once, and I didn't
like it at all.'

Amy thanked the man and then the small team trotted up the
three flights of stairs to the top floor. By the time they reached the
door, they could already hear the thumping bass of a stereo
coming from inside. Hunter had heard it as they walked up the
stairs, annoyed by how it gradually got louder and louder. He
shared a knowing look with his team and everyone knew this
could be what they were looking for.

Hunter banged on the door with a toe of his boot, but there
was no reply.

'They probably can't hear us,' Jodie said. 'How do these
assholes even hear themselves think when they make a noise like
this?'

'They don't do any thinking,' Blanco said.

Hunter banged on the door again but there was still no

response. Then he had an instinct to act but turned first to Blanco and Jodie. 'You two go back downstairs, go outside and see where the fire escapes are. Then, cover them. We'll go in heavy up here and if we don't catch them, we'll flush them out to you.'

'Got it,' Blanco said. 'C'mon, Jode!'

Hunter and Amy watched their friends vanish down the stairs and gave them enough time to get outside and make their way around the warehouse.

'Here goes nothing!' he said, raising his leg and kicking the door open with his boot, smashing it out of the lock and forcing it back against its hinges. He caught the scent of marijuana in the air and saw some needles lying around on the hall floor. It was that kind of place, he thought grimly. Then he just caught a glimpse of someone darting out of sight at the end of a corridor stretching out ahead of him.

'That's gotta be him!' Hunter said. 'And he's on the run.'

## 6

Hunter sprinted down the corridor, knowing Amy was a few yards behind him. When he reached the end, he turned right and saw a middle-spine staircase of grey metal ascending to the loft level. He charged up the stairs, craning his neck to make sure no one was waiting above for him, but when he got to the top, there was no one in sight. He was standing in a trendy loft space of exposed brick and wooden floorboards and saw with a sinking heart an open door leading to what looked like an external fire escape. The space was full of packing crates and old tea chests stacked high, pushed up against a sloping ceiling on both sides, forming a kind of central aisle.

Hunter headed towards the open door with Amy a few steps behind but was surprised when he felt a blow on the back of the head and fell onto the floor, eating floorboards and almost passing out. He looked up and saw a man with a baseball bat swinging it down towards his head as hard as he possibly could, and he only narrowly avoided a painful death by rolling out of the way. The bat hit the floor with a smack. Amy screamed and ran towards the man, but she was unarmed and was reduced to trying to force him away from Hunter with her bare hands.

The man reacted angrily, elbowing her in the face and forcing her back against some of the crates, which now teetered back and forth. Then he lifted the bat to try to strike Hunter a second time. Hunter was on his knees now and saw there was a kind of makeshift bedroom up here, using the crates as walls for privacy. He staggered to his feet and lunged towards the man, grabbing him around his waist and forcing him back through a gap in the crates onto an unmade bed. The man swung at him with the bat once again, but the angle was all wrong and he missed. Then Hunter punched the man in the face, knocking his head back against the side of the bed and disengaging from him, just in time to see Amy twisting the bat out of his hand and throwing it to the ground behind her.

The man managed to get to his feet, scrambling off the bed and slipping away along the aisle towards the open door. Hunter gave chase, running after him and throwing himself at him as he slowed to climb out of the window leading to the external fire escape. Hunter missed, but launched himself at the man once again, this time rugby-tackling him to the ground. The two men fought for a few moments, throwing punches and sometimes landing them before Hunter eventually subdued him.

'Tell me where we can find Oriax!' Hunter grabbed a fistful of the man's shirt and shook him hard.

'I will tell you nothing!' the man said in what Hunter believed was a thick Russian accent. 'You will never get to Oriax.'

'Yeah, we'll see about that, bastard,' Hunter said, shaking him again. 'You're going to tell me where he is because we need to know and he's obviously not here.'

'I see you are very clever,' the man said, a hint of sarcasm in his words. 'And yes, we understand all about you, Agent Fox and your many contacts in the FBI and CIA. But these contacts will not help you track down Oriax because he is too clever for you.'

'He's not clever enough to spoof his phone call properly,' Amy said as she walked slowly over to them. 'He could have made that telephone call appear from anywhere, but why here?'

The man smiled a deep, devilish grin that turned Hunter's blood to ice. As the English archaeologist ran Amy's words over in his mind, he realised something was terribly wrong.

'What's so funny?' he asked the man. 'Why are you smiling?'

The man now broke his arm free from Hunter's grip and brought his hand up to his mouth, quickly putting something inside it and crunching it between his teeth. Hunter watched in horror as foam began to bubble up out of the man's mouth and he went into a wild seizure, his body shaking violently under Hunter for a few moments before he finally died. As his head fell limply to the side, foam still bubbling out of his mouth onto the floorboards, Hunter leapt up from the man and cried out to Amy.

'We have to get out of here!'

'What's going on, Max?' Amy said. 'I don't understand. What did he say to you?'

'It's a trap!' Hunter said as he ran towards Amy and pulled her to the fire escape. 'The reason Oriax didn't hide the spoofed call better is because he wanted us here at this warehouse. It's booby-trapped. It's rigged to blow!'

Hunter didn't wait for Amy to respond and now dragged her to the fire escape, where the two of them began to make their way hastily down the black iron steps until finally reaching an alleyway at the side of the warehouse. When they reached it, Blanco and Jodie were running up towards them from round the back.

'What's going on, Max?' Blanco asked. 'Amy?'

'We have to get out of here immediately!' Hunter said. 'The place is rigged to blow!'

They ran towards the cab but were only halfway there when the entire top floor of the warehouse exploded in an enormous raging fireball of reds and oranges, spewing smoke and broken timber and glass and plastic and metal up into the air in a massive mushroom cloud before everything gradually fell to the ground all around them, landing on the asphalt with a tinkle and a clatter and a bang and a thud. Car alarms sounded everywhere, not only from the shockwave of the explosion but also large pieces of wood and other exploded material landing on them from so high, causing them to rock on their suspensions. People screamed all over the area, sprinting for the cover of the bridge or simply running away as fast as they could.

'We need to get out of here!' Blanco said, gesturing for the Black Cab to continue waiting for them, despite the obvious consternation of the driver.

'I'll buy that for a dollar.' Jodie was already making a move towards the cab. 'This place is going to be crawling with cops in seconds.'

Amy had also moved to join them when Hunter saw something on the ground. He reached down to pick it up, cursing and blowing on it because it was still hot from the explosion.

'What did you find?' Amy asked.

He shook his head. 'I'm not sure – maybe nothing. Let's just get out of here and then we can stop and have a look at it when we're safe.'

Hunter and the team got back into the cab and after batting away a few questions from the driver, they made their way down Camden High Street, the air now alive with the noise of emergency service sirens racing to the scene. Hunter knew London well enough to know that this would already have been registered somewhere as a possible terrorist attack, although the authorities would believe a more likely explanation was a simple gas explosion. Whether it was a terror attack or a gas explosion that was reported on the news would depend entirely on the government's COBRA meeting that would no doubt be called within the hour. Hunter could not remember the last time an entire warehouse blew up in the centre of London, and this would certainly be raising eyebrows in all the right places.

As they cruised slowly down the High Street, the driver switched on the radio and turned to a news station. There was already a report about the attack. The cabbie shook his head and lamented about what London had become, but Hunter's mind was focused closely on the mission. He looked at what he had picked up off the ground and prayed it could help them.

'What is that thing?' Jodie asked, leaning forward in her seat.

'Right now,' Hunter said, almost to himself, 'it's our only hope of finding Quinn and the others.'

## 7

By 10.30 a.m., Hunter was in a small café in King's Cross and St Pancras International Station. Following a quick discussion, the team had decided their journey was almost certain to involve leaving the United Kingdom, and this station was not only the home of the Eurostar train to Europe, but also on the Piccadilly Line, which would allow them to catch a Tube train straight to London Heathrow Airport.

Hunter was gently handling the item he had picked up back at the explosion, when Amy walked back over to their table from the counter. Blanco and Jodie had opted for simple cups of tea, but Amy had wanted an elaborate white chocolate mocha Frappuccino coffee that seemed to take longer to make than it took to grow and harvest the coffee beans. Hunter had confessed his love for Amy to Blanco not long ago, and watching her standing at the counter, he wondered exactly what would happen between them. Only time would tell.

When she returned, smiling with satisfaction after her first sip and sitting down beside Hunter, she wasted no time in getting down to business, as was her way.

'So, exactly what is that thing in your hands, Max?'

'It's a fragment of a detonator,' Hunter said.

He turned it in his hand and was reminded of the earliest part of his career when he was a Guards officer in the British Army. Items like handguns, rifles, grenades, explosives, blasting caps, and detonators had been something not central to his life as an officer but out on the periphery, especially after his initial training. He hadn't really come into close contact with these things regularly until he went on active duty in Iraq and Afghanistan. He understood exactly what he had seen down on the ground back in Camden, and he knew that it was the only chance they had of getting their own back on the psychopath who had deliberately led them to a building rigged with explosives.

'Detonators are always made of very sturdy, substantial materials so they can withstand the force of whatever they're being used to explode,' Hunter began. 'Very often after a devastating explosion – and I mean one set deliberately with explosives, not a gas leak or anything – some of the only objects remaining will be things like the detonator. The point is, this particular detonator has a partial serial number on it and the mark of a manufacturer that I don't recognise.'

'Gotcha,' Jodie said with a big smile on her face. 'You think you can use that serial number or manufacturer's mark as a lead?'

'I do.'

'That's a very sound idea,' Blanco said, nodding with approval.

Amy frowned. 'But you said you don't recognise it.'

'That's right,' Hunter said. 'I don't recognise it – that's not necessarily so surprising because I haven't been in the army for several years and they may have changed their supplier, but on the other hand, this particular serial number has a Continental 7 with a bar crossed through it, which usually means it was produced in mainland Europe. I know for a fact that our land mines, explosives, detonators and everything else are always produced by British defence contractors, so this is a little bit of a red flag for me.'

'You should've been a detective, Hunter,' Jodie said.

'That's kind of what an archaeologist is,' he replied. 'We have to look for leads and clues and follow the trail as much as we can, especially when we're out in the field. The tiniest fragment of information can tell you a whole lot more if you just sit down and think about it and follow where it leads you. I'm going to deduce right now that this detonator is made by a continental company, and was supplied – probably illegally – to Oriax and his little organisation, and then used to rig the warehouse.'

Jodie frowned. 'But what I don't understand is how they could have done that in the few hours it took for us to get there after Oriax's phone call?'

'You're not thinking laterally,' Amy said. 'Oriax clearly runs a major international criminal enterprise, and he will be heavily involved in trades like drug smuggling, weapons smuggling, and probably even people trafficking. He'll have several safe houses and warehouse distribution centres that he uses all over Europe and maybe even the world. I'm going to suggest that many of them, at least the ones that are holding the more dangerous and incriminating evidence, are already set with explosives. He led us there like lambs to the slaughter, letting us think we were being clever by getting George Pak to trace the spoofed call.'

'That's some 4D chess right there, man,' Jodie said.

Hunter agreed with Amy's reading of the situation. As a long-serving FBI agent, she would probably have the best under-standing on their team of a man like Oriax.

'I think that's exactly what happened,' Hunter said.

'So he spoofed the call to the warehouse in Camden on the

off-chance that he might be able to kill us when we got there, or at least slow us down,' Blanco said. 'I don't think I like this guy.'

'But what do we do about this detonator then?' Jodie asked.

Hunter had already taken out his telephone. 'I'm going to call an old friend of mine, he's an ex-soldier who retired a few months ago from the British Army. He made his way up through the ranks to lieutenant colonel and eventually worked in his last post as a quartermaster. I think he's the most likely person I know from the army who will be able to help us on this. I'm going to see if he knows anything about this manufacturer's mark. Just give me a second.'

Hunter pushed away from the table and walked outside the station. It was a cold fresh day in London with heavy cloud cover, and he pulled his collar up to deflect the wind that was whistling down the street from hitting his neck. At least it had stopped raining. He navigated to his contacts list, found his old friend and gave him a call.

'Mike, how are you doing?'

'Bloody good, mate. You?'

It was good to hear Mike Burton's voice after all these months. Hunter had most recently talked to him when he had left the army to wish him well in Civvy Street – he had not known then that he would be calling him on such an important matter so soon.

'I'm doing all right, all in all, Mike. Thanks for asking. I've got a bit of a problem though and was wondering if you could help me out?'

'Absolutely not. Fuck off!' Burton hung up.

Hunter wanted to smile at his old friend's humour, but the situation did not allow it. Now he called him up a second time and this time when he answered, Mike Burton could not stop himself from laughing.

'Sorry, mate, couldn't resist it. How can I help?'

'I'm trying to track down a weapons manufacturer, Mike. I've got a partial serial number and a manufacturer's mark on the side of a detonator and am very keen to work out who's trading in them at the moment because I don't think it's the British Army.'

'Now that sounds interesting,' Burton said. 'Give me the information.'

Hunter reeled off the partial serial number and then the manufacturer's mark, which he described in great detail – a kind of griffin with a cross behind it and then small stars in the spaces between the cross bars.

'Yeah, that's not anything to do with the British Army, Max. The lettering you describe, as you may know, is Russian. There's no way that anyone making that kind of stuff is supplying our boys. You have to give me more time to research the manufacturer's mark though.'

'Sure, how long do you need?' He felt frustrated that Mike had not been able to give him an answer immediately, but then that was always a longshot.

'Not long, mate,' Burton said cheerily. 'Need to make a few phone calls, that's all. I'll get back to you within fifteen minutes.'

Hunter was happy with that and went back inside the station where he spent the time chatting with his friends about old times, and their most recent experience at Tintagel Haven down in Cornwall. None of it seemed real to him, not even after all these years, but then he supposed that finding Atlantis was more than a fair warning about what the future of his life was to hold working with HARPA. His trip down memory lane with his old friends was interrupted by Burton returning his call.

'Mike, hi. Got something for me?'

'I surely do, old friend,' Burton said. 'The manufacturer is

Russian, as we suspected – Zlobin Industries – and they're based just outside St Petersburg, but that's not the interesting part.'

'And what might the interesting part be?' Hunter was keeping his voice low so as not to draw too much attention from the other people drinking and eating in the café all around him, but loud enough that his teammates could hear at least his half of the conversation.

'The interesting part is that Zlobin Industries not only supplies weapons to the Russian armed forces, but have also been known on occasion to 'accidentally' supply dealers on the black market. I have a friend of a friend of a friend, who has very obligingly passed a message back up the line. He says that a very large shipment of explosives and detonators, including the batch that would have contained the partial number that you have right there on your piece of evidence, was sent to a French black-market weapons trafficker by the name of Aristide Babineaux.'

Hunter made a note of the name. 'Go on, Mike.'

'By all accounts, Babineaux is an extremely unpleasant piece of work, but he has done so much trade with very senior figures, particularly in the French political ecosystem, that he has risen to extremely lofty heights. He lives in an enormous French chateau just on the outskirts of Paris, and apparently, he frequently hosts senior members of the French Cabinet and high-ranking business leaders in France. It is my friend's opinion that whoever left their detonator behind for you to find got that weapon from Babineaux.'

'That is extremely friendly and helpful of you, Mike,' Hunter said. 'I'll look forward to paying you back with half a lager at some point in the next ten years.'

'When did you get so generous?' Burton said.

'Only recently.'

'Half a lager, eh? I just knew I could count on you, old friend. And Max, one more thing.'

'What's that?'

'I don't know what you're up to these days besides your bone digging, but take it easy with this guy. I'm serious.'

'Thanks, buddy,' Hunter said. 'I'll see you around.'

Hunter hung up the call and slid the phone into his pocket before turning to his friends and explaining in not so many words what Mike Burton had just told him.

'Again, it's a bit thin,' Jodie said.

'But again,' Amy said, glancing at her, 'it's all we have.'

'Maybe it's all we need,' Blanco said, sipping his tea. 'As Max said earlier, this is a very different kind of mission for us. Not only do our usual skills not really apply here, but we don't even have Quinn, the one person who could help more than anyone else. We just have to kind of patch things together the best way we can and do our best to track down where they're holding her. Maybe this is how we do that. I think it's a good next step.'

'Exactly,' Hunter said. 'We know that Oriax deliberately spoofed the call through the warehouse in Camden so that we would go there. We also think the place was almost certainly previously rigged with explosives for other reasons, such as protecting their own merchandise in the event of a police raid or perhaps even an attack from another criminal rival organisation. Then his deranged minion kills himself and detonates the place, almost taking us all with him.'

'Risky though,' Blanco said. 'Oriax had no idea if the sword would get damaged in the blast.'

'Something tells me he knows the sword was never in any danger,' Amy said.

Hunter agreed. 'He was probably planning on having one of his minions pulling it out of the wreckage. Anyway, now we're left with this small piece of bent metal and a few scratchy marks on it. I think we've done pretty well so far, all in all.'

'Yeah, well... less of the hubris,' Jodie said. 'All we've got is the address of a French chateau and we've already been warned that the guy who lives in it is probably a total psychopath.'

'Yes,' Hunter said, 'but he's probably a total psychopath who is doing business with Oriax, and that's our way to find him and Quinn and the rest of our friends. I'm going to make another call.'

'To whom?' Amy asked.

'I'm booking us on the Eurostar. We're going to take the train to Paris. It'll be quicker than buggering around at two different airports at the beginning and end of the flight.' Hunter checked his watch. 'It's 10.45 a.m. now and there's a Eurostar train leaving at half past eleven. If we take that, I think we can be in Paris by around 2.50 p.m. local time. Everybody, pack your phrasebooks.'

'I'd rather pack a gun,' Jodie said.

## 8

Amy Fox had never been to St Pancras Railway Station before and was quietly impressed by the beauty of the twenty-five iron trusses supporting the enormous glass roof high above her. Since 2007, they had been painted powder blue to match their original colour back when the station was built in the 1860s. According to the quick research she had done on her phone on the Underground train over to the station, each one of these trusses weighed fifty-five tons and allowed the station to be filled with light, even on a dull day like today.

Hunter now walked over to her, waving his phone. He had bought the four Eurostar tickets and was disappointed that instead of a beautiful paper affair, he had nothing more than a QR code to show for his money. She smiled at just how amusingly old-fashioned he could be, and then the four of them made their way through to the departure lounge where they could see the enormous Eurostar train idling on the tracks just alongside the platform.

'I've never been to Paris on the train before,' Amy said. 'It seems kind of romantic.'

Jodie rolled her eyes and disappeared into her smartphone.

Blanco nodded and agreed then turned his attention to the departures board on the wall of the lounge.

'Have you made the trip on the train before?' Amy asked Hunter.

'Yes, I have,' he said. 'Twenty years ago now. My recollection of it is dim, but I do remember that the British end of the journey was slow and uncomfortable, and then things speeded up in the tunnel before going absolutely nuts on the French side. It was kind of embarrassing. I'm hoping they've sorted that out.'

'I see you're not a big fan of British rail infrastructure,' Blanco said with a smile.

Hunter smiled back. 'I'm a big fan of British railway infrastructure, it's just a shame that the people responsible for it clearly are not.'

Blanco huffed out a laugh. 'I haven't ridden the rails since I got a train from San Bernardino into downtown LA. My God, that must have been nearly thirty years ago. It was okay if I'm being honest. A double-decker kind of thing. I sat downstairs. I drank a Coke.'

'Thank you for that, Sal,' Amy said, nodding appreciatively. 'It's these small details that make this team just seem to come alive for me.'

'Yeah,' Jodie said, still looking at her phone. 'They really make things pop up into 3D.'

'Hey, you weren't even born when I was drinking that Coke on that train,' Blanco said, his face beaming at the memory. 'I was a young man. I'd driven a car across America for a friend, all the way from Memphis, Tennessee to San Bernardino. I dropped the car off and he was pretty happy to have it at last, so then he drove me to the station and I decided to hop a freight car... Or I would have done if I was Kerouac. In fact, I sat in coach and read the newspaper. And drank a Coke.'

Amy was smiling at Jodie's reaction more than Blanco's trip down memory lane, but then Hunter got up and suggested they all move across the platform to the train. As usual, it was a busy morning in St Pancras station and they had to fight their way through the crowd before finally boarding the train. It was more luxurious than Hunter had remembered and the four of them sat around a table in a nice temperature-controlled, clean environment. He was secretly looking forward to taking the train all the way to Paris; he enjoyed it much more than the prospect of flying. He had flown Apaches a long time ago after leaving his Guards regiment and joining the Army Air Corps, but these days he preferred to stay out of the sky as much as possible.

When the train finally pulled out of the station, a sense of childish excitement grew within him, and he watched out of the window as the station disappeared behind them and the graffitied walls and rooftops and TV aerials of London began to slowly go past them.

Amy closed her eyes and rested her head on the seat behind her, allowing the smooth, rocking motion of the locomotive to lull her into a light doze. It turned out she had gone much deeper than a light doze, and when she opened her eyes, the train was now in the tunnel and the London landscape had been replaced by a big rectangle of black and her own reflection looking back at her.

'How long have I been asleep for?' she asked, staring at her watch.

'Not long,' Hunter said. 'Around an hour or so.'

Jodie grinned. 'But in that time, Max managed to draw one of those little pointy beards and moustaches on your face with a black marker pen.'

Amy smiled, but Jodie's joke had been ruined by the fact that the first thing she had seen when opening her eyes was her own reflection in the window. She reached into her bag, in search of a bottle of water that had been chilled when she had bought it from the vending machine on the platform but was now almost room temperature.

'Any news about Ben's son, by the way?' Blanco asked Amy.

'Not last time I checked.'

The team fell silent for a few seconds, each privately hoping their friend's baby would pull through. Amy checked her phone again, but it was in vain. Then she started to unscrew the lid of her water bottle when she noticed a man walking menacingly towards them. He was in a long black coat but was wearing a bright white T-shirt underneath it. He had shoulder-length brown, wavy hair, a tanned face, and bright blue eyes that were his most striking feature. She was fixed on the eyes until she saw him pull a knife from his pocket and run over to their table.

She screamed. Blanco and Jodie, who were sitting opposite her, both turned in their seats but it was Hunter who reacted first, putting his right hand on the table to climb over the top of her and landing with a thud in the aisle between the two rows of seats. She watched in horror as Hunter grappled with the man, knocking the knife from his hand and twisting his arm behind his back before wheeling him around to their table and slamming him down onto it. Then with his other hand, he pushed the man's head down into Blanco's sandwich, squeezing the filling out from between the slices of bread and squashing it up all over his face.

'Just who the hell are you?' Hunter asked.

The man grunted something incoherent, his accent making him hard to understand.

Amy's FBI training kicked in and kept her calm, but she was shocked at the speed with which the man had appeared from nowhere and tried to attack them. Blanco had stood up as far as he was able behind the little table and was now leaning on the man, helping Hunter to keep him down. Jodie had slipped out as she was sitting on the aisle side and now picked up the man's knife, walking back to the table and putting it in her pocket.

'I asked who you were?' Hunter said. 'And I advise that you tell me before I break your arm.'

An elderly couple who were sitting at the table opposite them now looked at them in horror, got up and walked away to the next carriage. Amy realised that no one else in the carriage could see them from where they were sitting, but the tussle between Hunter and the man who had approached them had drawn a certain amount of attention, and now she saw a young couple down at the end of the carriage also walk away.

'Hurry up, Max,' she said. 'Maybe these guys might get a guard or something.'

'Who are you?' Hunter repeated.

'My name is Simeon. I belong to the Guild of St Michael.'

His words hit Amy like a sledgehammer. 'As in the Archangel Michael?'

'Yes!' the man spat out angrily. 'As in the Archangel Michael. I am here today to assassinate you and stop you from giving the Sword of the Archangel Michael to Oriax and his Illuminati scum.'

'Well, you didn't do a very good job of it, did you?' Jodie asked.

Amy felt the table shake as the man struggled to release himself, but the weight of Hunter and Blanco pushing down on him was just too much. He was trapped there until they decided to release him.

'You must return the sword to me and let me take it back to the Guild!' the man said.

'Wait a minute – just how the hell do you know who we are and that we have the sword?' Hunter asked.

'The sword should never have been released from its resting place, but when I saw the murder of those people at Tintagel Haven on the news, I knew it had been found. My superiors in the Guild ordered me to track you down and take the sword. You are to be killed for your part in the desecration of such a holy relic!'

'Desecration?' Hunter said. 'I'm an archaeologist! I don't desecrate holy relics. I discover them. I look after them. I catalogue them. I keep them safe for future generations.'

'You mean like trying to give the sword to Oriax? Is that what you call not being sacrilegious?'

'We're not going to actually give the sword to Oriax, you fool,' Jodie said. 'We lied to him so we can get our friends back.'

The man seemed to relax and accept his fate.

Amy felt sorry for him despite the fact he had tried to kill her with a knife just moments before. 'Max, I don't think he's dangerous. I think you should let him go so we can talk properly.'

'He tried to stab us with a knife, Amy!' Hunter said. 'He's not going anywhere till we get to France and the police can take him away.'

'I think this is a big mistake,' Simeon said.

'Well... you would, wouldn't you?' Hunter said, pushing down on him once again and making him grunt in pain.

'If we let you go, will you sit with us and talk or will you try to kill us again?' Amy asked. 'Be careful how you answer, because these guys can keep you like this all the way to Paris.'

'Yeah, we can,' Hunter said.

Blanco looked slightly less committed. 'I don't know, actually... The bottom of my back's starting to give me real trouble.'

Simeon sighed. 'Yes, I give you my most solemn promise I will not try to kill you. But I will make no further promises, especially about the sword!'

Hunter and Blanco released Simeon. They rearranged the seating, so Hunter and Simeon were sitting at the table opposite, where the old couple had been and Blanco, Amy and Jodie were sitting at their original table, so when they spoke they spoke across the aisle.

'Is the sword in that backpack?' Simeon asked, nodding to Blanco's bag.

Jodie said, 'No.'

'There's no point in lying to him,' Amy said. 'You already heard him – he belongs to some Guild devoted to St Michael. He knew it was in Tintagel. So, yes. The sword is in that bag.'

'Could I see it?' Simeon asked, his eyes beginning to shine brightly. 'Could I touch it?'

'It'll be staying exactly where it is for now, thank you very much,' Hunter said.

'It would mean a great deal to me,' Simeon said. 'More than my life.'

Amy nodded. 'Show it to him, but keep it out of the other passengers' sight.'

'Sure thing.' Blanco unzipped his pack and carefully withdrew the sword. It was wrapped in a cream linen pillowcase liberated from the Cornish hotel, which he now slowly unfolded, revealing the ancient relic to the eyes of the modern world one more time. 'What d'ya think?'

Simeon was speechless. He held out his hands to receive the sword, and after another nod from Amy, Blanco handed it over. The young Frenchman took the heavy weapon in his hands and stared at it with awe. He mumbled something in his mother tongue and then focused his attention on the inscription: *Gladius Sancti Michaelis.*

'The sword of St Michael! So, it is true.'

'We're sure of it,' Hunter said. 'But we're not sure what the symbols mean. There's someone back in England, someone named Lauren...' When he uttered Lauren's name, he caught a vaguely disapproving look from Amy, but continued. 'She's a very talented archaeologist specialising in this period and she's trying to translate them for us.'

'In this period?' Simeon said.

'The time of King Arthur,' Hunter replied. 'We think this was also Excalibur.'

'That may be so, and I have heard that theory many times, but these symbols are not from the time of King Arthur. No, these symbols were not carved into the sword by Arthur. The Guild believes these symbols – unintelligible to me – were created when the sword was originally forged.'

'For St Michael?' Amy asked.

Simeon nodded. 'Indeed.'

'But that would mean...' Blanco said, his words trailing away into the soft hum of the speeding carriage.

'That this sword was not forged by human hands,' Simeon said, almost in a whisper, his words even and reverential. 'This sword was the flaming sword of the Archangel Michael, created by God himself.'

Hunter looked down at the shining blade, reflecting in the muted overhead cabin light and found what Simeon had just said to be utterly believable. It was, aesthetically, the most beautiful sword he had ever seen, and his work for UNESCO had been generous to him in that regard, especially on digs in ancient Greece and Rome. He had presumed the main blade was steel, but considering what Simeon had just said, and the pale rosy glow in the metal, he was now thinking the possibility of an alloy of steel and orichalcum, the strange metal Plato had described as coming from Atlantis. It wouldn't surprise him. The rest of the sword was just as impressive, with the same rose-coloured metal used for the crossguard, and a pommel forged in the shape of a star.

'Why is there a star on the pommel?' Jodie asked.

'Obviously a reference to Arcturus,' Hunter said. 'The brightest star in the Boötes constellation which just happens to be where the name Arthur comes from. As I just said, we believe this was also King Arthur's Excalibur.' He turned to Jodie. 'You're welcome.'

Simeon looked from Hunter to Jodie. 'And you're also wrong if you believe that!'

Hunter frowned. 'Eh?'

'This star has nothing to do with Arthur!' the Frenchman said defiantly. 'This is a falling star! It represents the expulsion of Lucifer from heaven.'

'Too bad, Hunter,' Jodie said with a grin. 'Close, but definitely no cigar for you.'

Before Hunter could reply, Simeon went on. 'The expulsion of the angel Lucifer from heaven was the sword's first and mightiest battle... unless the prophecy is fulfilled.'

Hunter looked to Amy first, and then the others all exchanged concerned glances.

'Prophecy?' Amy asked. 'What prophecy?'

Simeon looked shocked. 'You have the Archangel's sword but you do not know about the angel prophecy?'

After a pause, Hunter spoke. 'You seem to have the advantage.'

'Can you tell us about it, please?' Amy asked.

Simeon's expression turned from shock to something approaching embarrassment. 'I know very little about it, I'm sorry. The prophecy is known only by the mentor.'

'The mentor?' Jodie asked. 'Sounds serious.'

'He is serious enough,' Simeon said. 'He is the leader of the Guild, and the prophecy is only ever entrusted to the leader. All I can tell you is that there is a prophecy attached to this sword, a terrible prophecy foretelling how the wielder of this blade will become as powerful as God. I wish I could tell you more.'

Blanco shifted in his seat. 'I'm sort of glad you can't.'

Simeon managed a smile, but it soon faded. 'Please, take this sword and keep it safe. The future of the world depends on it.'

After a short moment of reflection, Blanco took the weapon, wrapped it back up in the pillowcase and returned it to his pack. Amy was the first to speak.

'Simeon, I think now we showed you the sword, you can return the gesture by telling us who exactly this Guild of St Michael is and what your part in all of this is.'

'Very well,' Simeon said. 'The Guild of St Michael is an ancient society formed many hundreds of years ago with the explicit purpose of protecting the sword. You must know there are very important religious reasons for this. You are lucky that we have turned today into a day of talk and not war. My duty was to kill you all and take the sword.'

'Do you believe us about not wanting to give the sword to Oriax?' Amy said.

'I have no choice at this exact time other than to believe you, but if you betray me, the Guild will send more after you!'

'I hope they're better than you,' Jodie said.

'Yes,' Simeon said. 'They are better than me. On this occasion we underestimated you. We are not a big organisation with limit-less resources. What we can learn about people is limited. We believed you to be an archaeologist, a thief, a retired soldier who wants to make pizzas and an FBI agent. I did not anticipate such quick reactions from you, Dr Hunter.'

'You can call me Max,' Hunter said. 'All my friends do and you know I'd like to count you among my friends if that's okay because some of my very closest friends often approach me wielding a knife and try and stab me in the stomach with it.'

'I was trying to protect the sword!' Simeon grew angry. 'You have no idea how dangerous Oriax can be!'

'Yeah, I think we do,' Amy said. 'He's kidnapped several of our closest friends and he tried to kill us a few hours ago with an explosion at a converted warehouse. We're beginning to form a good opinion of Oriax.'

'You only know the very beginnings of it,' Simeon said. 'He is a very evil and warped man and I can't imagine why he wants the Sword of St Michael. He must have read some depraved or wicked thing he can do with it if he gets his hands on it. That must never happen! And there is more, much more. It is not just your friends whose fate it was to be kidnapped by Oriax. Some moments ago, I mentioned my mentor, Professor Jacques Toussaint, but there was something I never told you. Just a few days ago, he was also snatched by Oriax and his henchmen. Oriax is demanding the Guild stop trying to take the sword or he will be killed.'

'My God,' Blanco said. 'Oriax has kidnapped another person?'

Simeon nodded glumly. 'Professor Toussaint is an old man, a great, learned man. He has run the Guild for years. I fear for his life.'

'Why doesn't the Guild go and bust him out?' Jodie asked. 'If you're so tough, I mean.'

Simeon fell silent, his eyes dropping to the floor. 'I lied about all of that. There is a Guild, but we are tiny. There are only a handful of us. We are an academic organisation, mere amateurs compared with Oriax. I cannot get Professor Toussaint back.'

Without consulting the rest of the team, Amy now fixed Simeon in the eyes. 'Why don't we work together?'

Simeon looked surprised, but not as shocked as Hunter, Blanco and Jodie.

'Are you crazy?' Jodie asked. 'We can't trust this guy! He could be absolutely anybody. He just tried to kill us. He could be spinning us any bullshit story and you're just going to swallow it hook, line and sinker?'

'Hey!' Amy said, her tone growing angry and vaguely maternal. 'Don't you forget I'm the leader of this team and I'll make the calls.'

Jodie shrugged and sank back down into her chair, once again pulling her phone up and navigating to something of significantly more interest to her than the current conversation.

'Anyone else got a problem with that?' Amy asked.

Hunter and Blanco both shook their heads vaguely, and Amy turned her attention back to Simeon.

'It's something about your eyes, Simeon, but I know you're one of the good guys. You only tried to attack us because you thought we were going to hand the sword over to Oriax. Well, we're not going to. We're going to make them think that until we've got our friends back and then we're going to end Oriax once and for all. We'll help you get your mentor back.'

'Hey,' Hunter said. 'Aren't you forgetting we have a deadline?'

'No, I am not. But we can't let Oriax execute an innocent professor.'

'If he's even real,' Jodie muttered.

Amy sighed. 'Plus this way, we get Simeon fighting with us.'

'And we've all seen how good he is,' Jodie said.

Amy turned to the Frenchman. 'Shall we work together?'

Simeon considered in silence for a few moments, then he

nodded his head. 'But you must return the sword to the Guild at the end of this battle! We have protected it for centuries.'

'Looks like we have a deal,' Hunter said.

Then the train burst out of the tunnel and the cabin was filled with blinding bright, fresh sunshine. Outside, the rolling pastoral hills of northern France unfolded all the way to the horizon, a much bigger horizon than they had left behind in Kent. Amy looked from Simeon's eyes to the view outside and then across to the bag where the sword was hidden. She was suddenly much more enthusiastic and optimistic about the mission.

She just hoped that feeling wasn't misplaced.

## 9

Quinn Mosley knew two things above all else – she had to stay alive and she had a duty to try to escape. She couldn't rely on the others to come and get her so she had to do this on her own, but there was a problem. She had no idea where she was, or even who had taken her. The last thing she remembered was being in a car parked up in a forest where she thought she was safe, then they had struck like lightning. She was hooded and knocked out. She woke up on an aircraft flying in the air, not parked on the ground.

When she thought about what happened back in the forest, she felt sick all over again. Shadows moving in the trees. A man in black smashed the car window she was sitting in with a rock, covering her in broken glass. Not giving a damn if the shards cut her eyes. She remembered screaming as his big long arm reached into the car and unlocked the door. He wore black leather gloves and had large meaty, strong hands. She tried to fight back but she stood no chance.

Another man had appeared on the other side of the car, somewhere out in the trees. He came to the car and fired a gun at the petrol tank just as the first man had heaved her free from it and got her away from the vehicle. The car exploded in the woods; she could still feel the shockwave blasting against her face. Then it all went black. She woke on a plane and a man called Jophiel had spoken to her and told her they were flying over the North Atlantic. He had talked to her about a man he called the High Lord of his society. He had told her that meant Illuminati. She had not really believed him. There was something about it that didn't ring true.

After that, things had grown dim again. There had been another hood and more drugs. She had washed in and out of consciousness so much that she was starting to feel completely unreal. The world also felt unreal, as if everything was no more than a dream. She had heard nothing from the HARPA team since she had said goodbye to them in the forest, but she had no idea how long ago that was. Now she was sitting in what looked like some kind of basement, and she was able to deduce from the power sockets in the wall that she was in North America, but that was all she had.

Then a door at the top of a short flight of wooden steps opened to reveal a large silhouette of a man standing at the top, looking down at her. She felt fear; she wasn't conceited enough to deny that much, but she also felt defiance and resilience. No one in the HARPA team really knew anything about her past, but she was able to draw on some of that experience to deal with what was standing before her now. She surely had faced more menacing foes in her experience with HARPA than was standing at the top of this flight of steps right now. After all, if they wanted her dead, they'd had several opportunities to satisfy their desire since kidnapping her. She was alive for a reason, although she could not depend on that reason lasting permanently.

'Hey, Jophiel! How's it going?' She tried to sound casual and not alarmed in any way, but she was not sure she had pulled that off. 'How's it hanging? That is you, isn't it, Jophiel?'

The man at the top of the stairs made his way slowly down each step one by one until he hit the bottom. Then he walked towards her, his footsteps clicking on the polished concrete and echoing in the basement all around her. When he reached the bottom, he put his hands in his pockets and strolled casually over to her.

'Yes, it is Jophiel,' the man said. 'I do hope you are enjoying our hospitality?'

'Sure I am,' Quinn said, looking around the dark gloomy basement. 'I especially like the way you leave your guests to sit on cold concrete for several hours. You should go into the hospitality business.'

'An attempt at humour to soften your grim predicament,' Jophiel said, almost to himself. 'An entirely expected response. Unfortunately, not all of your band of merry hostages are as calm and collected as you are, Agent Mosley. Jim Gates is doing all right, but it's taking quite a lot of his persuasive talents to keep his wife Susanna calm, and Professor Bonnaire hasn't stopped muttering to herself in French since we kidnapped her.'

Quinn was shocked. 'You kidnapped Jim and Susanna Gates and Juliette Bonnaire as well?'

'We're keeping the Gateses together in another basement and Bonnaire is separate, like you.'

Quinn felt hope draining from her heart. 'Why have you done this, Jophiel?'

'I have done nothing except follow the orders of my master.'

'Oh, yeah – real good,' Quinn said, her voice dripping with sarcasm as she tried to rally herself. 'The Nuremberg defence. Great work.'

'I'm not interested in your asinine opinions on how I conduct my life or how I play my part in our glorious institution. We all have a part to play in this world, Agent Mosley. Yours is in your dubious HARPA team. Mine is a part of the world's most glorious secret society, the Illuminati.'

'I thought you didn't like that word?' Quinn asked, remembering when they had first kidnapped her and Jophiel had referred to the Illuminati as 'lowbrow'.

'I use it for simplicity, making allowances for the person to whom I am speaking.'

Quinn paused before replying. 'Why am I down here? I mean, you bastards kidnapped me from that forest, put me on a plane, flew me across an ocean and then I wake up in here after being drugged for like the zillionth time. What the hell is going on?'

'You are collateral in a very serious business deal, and that is all you are. You and the rest of the hostages are being held until the master receives the Sword of the Archangel Michael. When he receives it, you will be released.'

'You can't promise me that, Jophiel. If he ever gets his hands on that sword, we'll all be dead within the hour.'

'That is for the master to decide.'

'They'll never give it to you, you know,' Quinn said, once again sounding defiant. 'They'll never give it to you, no matter what you threaten.'

'You really think your friends would let you die over an ancient relic, of which they know not the first thing? Perhaps I think a little more highly of them than you do.'

'I don't know what they'll do,' Quinn said, feeling confused all of a sudden. She knew HARPA would never give Jophiel or his master in the Illuminati the Archangel's Sword, but on the other hand, she knew they would do everything in their power to stop her and the Gateses and Professor Bonnaire being murdered.

'Whatever they'll do, your so-called master won't get that sword.'

'We shall see about that,' Jophiel said. 'Master has already spoken with HARPA and agreed to make a trade.'

'I don't believe it.'

'I don't care whether you believe it or not, but that is the case. They have already agreed with the master and we will be trading the sword for your lives in less than a day.' Jophiel's voice softened and now he crouched down so they were eye to eye. 'Quinn – you don't mind if I call you Quinn, do you?'

Quinn shrugged. 'Knock yourself out.'

'I like you, Quinn. I think you're intelligent and brave. I like Jim and Susanna Gates and I like Professor Bonnaire. We're not all lunatic psychopaths in the Illuminati, you realise. My master has a vision for the world, but he is not a bad man. I don't believe he will kill you if your friends hand over the sword.'

'But you can't be sure.'

Jophiel scratched his cheek and rose back up to his feet. 'No, I can't be sure and I can't make you any promises.'

Quinn was even more confused now. This man had shown her little mercy when she had woken up on the aircraft immediately after being kidnapped, but now his voice seemed calmer and warmer and she sensed a genuine compassion in his words, even if it was just the slightest ounce, the slightest shred. She made a note that maybe Jophiel could become a strange sort of ally and might be able to help her out in this dire situation she found herself in.

'Where is your master meeting my team to do the trade?'

'That is not of your concern,' Jophiel said, his voice growing terser and colder. 'But we will be making another flight. You will be drugged for the entire duration of the flight. I'm sorry, but that is out of my hands. The master has decided that you and the others must not know any of the locations in which you have been held, in case any of you manage to escape. These are all secure Illuminati facilities and they will remain entirely secret from the world.'

Quinn watched Jophiel turn on his heel and walk back to the stairs. At the bottom of the steps, he turned and faced her once again, although now his face was made dark by the light coming from the top of the steps.

'I'll do what I can to keep the four of you alive.'

Before Quinn had a chance to say thanks, he rattled up the steps and slammed the door behind him. Then she heard a key turn in the lock and her world was once again dark and silent. She quietly and inwardly prayed that Amy Fox, Max Hunter, Sal Blanco and Jodie Priest would be able to locate her and save her life before Jophiel's deranged master decided to end it.

## 10

The Gare du Nord was as Hunter had expected to find it – busy, noisy, but still somehow charming in that particular French way that he found so irresistible. After a few minutes at customs, they made their way to the exit. The afternoon sun was streaming into the station, and he could barely believe that he had started the day in Cornwall, travelled to London and was now being welcomed by the city of lights – a city with a special place in his heart, thanks to a serious relationship with Avril, a Parisienne he had almost married. It didn't take them long to find the private SUV Amy had hired while travelling across northern France, and they were soon sitting in the spacious luxury of an eight-seater V-Class Mercedes, trundling north out of the French capital on their way to the small town of Bouqueval.

They passed a university at Saint-Denis and cruised through Arnouville before finally breaking out of the massive grey metropolis and for a short while, riding along a stretch of road flanked on both sides by soft countryside. It was a view Hunter always enjoyed, seeing the traditional French farmhouses with their shuttered windows, and the slightly peculiar way French farms divided their fields up – owing to the ancient French inheritance laws that demanded farmland was broken up equally between sons, rather than left only to one as was the case traditionally in England.

Hunter also spent much of the journey keeping an eye on their newest recruit, the mysterious Simeon. He said nothing for most of the trip, and sat with his eyes closed and a peaceful look on his face. He looked younger now, finally presented with a way to rescue his mentor. If any of his story was true, Hunter mulled. It wasn't long before they reached Goussainville and after pulling up on a small road leading away from the town to the west they climbed out of the SUV and asked their driver to wait for them and keep out of sight. The sky had cleared and the bright French sunshine was shining down on their faces for the first time since they had arrived in Paris.

'It's a five-minute walk from here,' Amy said, once again consulting her phone. 'Just to the east. We should see the chateau soon enough. It'll be off just to our right in the north somewhere, just outside of Bouqueval.'

'Pretty nice place to have a chateau, if you ask me,' Blanco said, still carrying the backpack containing the sword.

Hunter was thinking exactly the same thing. He was something of a Francophile and had secretly wished one day to retire to France, although a little further south than here if possible. He wanted to buy himself one of those old rambling farmhouses with dubious electrics and even worse plumbing that he could then spend his twilight years slowly bringing back to life. In Hunter's case, that dream usually involved him sitting on a bench under a flowered trellis, practising his French with a copy of *Le Figaro* while watching a team of hard-working tradesmen somewhere off in the distance, repairing his roof and fixing the well.

He thought that with some effort and practice, he would be

able to adjust to such a life, but whether or not Amy was up for it he didn't know. The two of them had been very close in recent times, and she had shown no sign of wanting to leave the United States at all. Her life was there, including family and former work colleagues, and although he had never mentioned the subject to her, he was pretty sure what the answer would be if he raised it. He could live without it, too. Hunter loved the United States and always had done. He liked to make jokes about Americans, but he saw it in the way a brother makes fun of another brother. The idea of him and Amy maybe one day getting married and buying a rural farmhouse somewhere in the northeast also appealed to him, although he would never tolerate American spelling or their completely incorrect views on British cooking. Hunter always found the American mockery of British cooking and music rather odd, considering they were the inventors of chilli dogs and cheese in a spray can, but he conceded they might have a point when it came to British dentistry.

The short walk through the fields was pleasant owing to the bright, warm sunshine that had come out when they got out of the Mercedes at Goussainville. They walked along the outer side of the fields on a public footpath. Hunter was not exactly sure of the law in France, but back home in England this would have been a public right of way at common law. He guessed it didn't matter too much as they were about to break into a chateau, which they now saw through a break in a line of beautiful glistening plane trees off to their right. It was an enormous ego-busting French architectural display that looked as if it had not been built so much as created elsewhere and then lowered down into the landscape by a crane. It had an almost bluish tint to its tiled roof, more round towers and turrets than it probably needed, and literally countless numbers of windows reflecting the sunshine at him. Behind it, there were some low hills carpeted in oaks and ash trees and maybe some chestnuts. In front was a broad expansive formal lawn with some topiary on it and what looked to him like a maze cut out of yew trees.

'Who says the rich don't know how to have fun?' Blanco said.

'Yeah, he must have a lot of fun in that maze when he's not killing people,' Jodie said.

'Maybe Babineaux kills people in the maze?' Blanco said with a shrug. 'You never know.'

'Indeed,' Simeon said. 'I am sure many people will have been killed right here on this property. I will soon bring justice to him if he has played any part in the kidnapping of Professor Toussaint.'

Hunter turned to face the Frenchman. This was pretty much the first full sentence he had said since embarking the RER commuter train in Paris. 'Hey, just take it easy there, okay, Simeon? We don't want any heroics. Only I do the heroics. That is a long-established tradition in this team.'

Hunter noticed Amy gave him a sideways look. 'What? Just saying how it is.'

'I take exception to that, Hunter,' Jodie said. 'If you look back through our history together, I'm the one that does the hero stuff.'

Hunter smiled and considered this was quite possibly true, but there were few things as enjoyable as getting a rise out of Jodie Priest, so he was glad he had said it.

They continued up the lane towards the chateau until they reached a set of large ornate iron gates, and just behind them was a small gatehouse. Hunter noticed a moment too late that there was a camera in the eaves of the gatehouse and before any of them had the chance to respond to it, a man in a security uniform stepped out of the gatehouse door and walked over to them. He was carrying a radio and remained behind the iron gates.

'*Que faites-vous tous ici?*' he asked and repeated in English when he saw their blank faces staring back at him. 'What are you doing here?'

'We've come to see Monsieur Babineaux,' Hunter said, replying in English although he had understood the French.

'He has no appointments today. Please leave.'

Hunter reached into his pocket and pulled out the fragment of the detonator. He held it up so the man was able to see clearly the Russian manufacturer's mark. 'The thing is, I want to talk to him about business, and I think he'll see us even if we don't have an appointment.'

The man looked suspicious for a moment, his eyes crawling all over Hunter and the rest of the team. He had already looked at the griffin on the detonator but now he leaned in to take a closer look at the serial numbers. Hunter thought he did not really understand what he was looking at, but it was enough to make him bring the radio to his face and connect with someone back up at the chateau. A flurry of French words raced past them like a whirling dervish and then before they knew what had happened, the man walked back to the gatehouse and then they heard a buzz and the gates began to swing open mechanically.

When they stepped through the gates, the man came up to them, this time armed with a handgun which he waved in their faces.

'Hands in the air.'

None of the team was armed so they were all happy to do as he asked and after a quick pat down, the man made another call in French. He received his reply in a blazing crackle of static which none of them had a chance of understanding. Then he fixed his eye on Hunter and told them that they were to walk up the main drive where they would be met outside the house.

'Well, that was easy,' Blanco said.

'Getting into shit is always easy,' Jodie said. 'It's getting out of it where the trouble starts.'

'Not for you guys,' Amy said, lowering her voice. 'I want you to wait out here, Sal, with the sword. If anything happens and we're not back in say, thirty minutes, then you go and get somewhere safe. Here's my phone – in case Oriax calls.'

Blanco took the phone but looked unhappy at the thought of letting his teammates go into the chateau without him. 'I'm not so sure about this, Amy. First, you could really need me in there, and second, what good can I do for Quinn if you're all dead?'

'You can get her back with the sword.'

'Sure, if it's not a trap.'

'We can't plan for everything, Sal.' Amy turned to Jodie. 'I want you out here, too.'

'Got it.'

Amy turned to Hunter and Simeon. 'It's show time.'

## 11

They were met at the door by two significantly more serious-looking men than the security guard back at the gatehouse. On their way towards them, as they walked up the central pathway, Hunter decided that they were almost certainly ex-military and clearly part of Babineaux's close protection squad. One of them was blond, with bright blue eyes, in his thirties and tall but powerful looking. The other was squat, olive-skinned with short curly brown hair and dark brown eyes, and when Hunter looked at him he was strangely reminded of one of those sides of beef you see hanging up in butchers' windows.

'Hands up!' the blond man said.

'We just did all that down there at the gatehouse,' Hunter said. 'Is it really necessary to go through it all again?'

'Just put your damn hands up,' the man said in a heavy Russian accent. 'Is protocol.'

Hunter and the rest of the team followed the man's orders and raised their hands. Another slightly more invasive body search went by and then the man turned to the side of beef and spoke not in French but in Russian. He wasn't able to catch what was said, but Hunter could deduce it easily enough when both of the men stepped aside and ordered them to go up into the house's main entrance.

Hunter stepped through some large oak double doors into a beautiful decorative lobby area with a black and white tiled floor, carved wooden hall chairs running around the outside of the room, and a beautiful display of Baroque and classical art that would make many small galleries jealous. An enormous chandelier dominated the air above their heads and drew Hunter's attention up to a beautifully ornate ceiling fifty feet above them.

'Wait here,' said the blond man. 'If you like, you can share some jokes with my friend.'

Hunter watched the blond-haired man walk through a door and close it firmly behind him. Turning to the man with brown curly hair, he smiled.

'You like jokes then? How about this one. Yesterday, my wife told me there was someone at the door with an ugly face and I said, tell him you've already got one.'

'Shut up,' said the guard.

'Yeah, shut up,' Amy said.

Hunter took her advice. He had no idea what to expect in this place, especially after his friend Mike Burton had warned him about how dangerous Babineaux could be. Hunter wasn't here to challenge Babineaux or threaten him or blackmail him. He just wanted information and he wondered if he had a half decent chance of getting it, but he wasn't above threats or blackmail if he had to.

The door opened and the blond man stepped back into the hallway.

'Follow me,' he said.

Hunter and Amy shared a quick glance and then walked with Simeon across the hall, following the blond man through the door where they found a smaller vestibule leading to a grand hallway. They turned into the hall, which hosted a large dark-wood staircase twisting up ahead of them. The blond man walked up the stairs and as they followed him, Hunter was hyper aware of each old wooden step creaking under his weight. Passing yet more beautiful oil paintings hanging on walls of blood-coloured damask wallpaper, time slowed to a crawl and he felt unexpect-edly vulnerable in the oppressive atmosphere of the old house. The chateau had an eerie character that Hunter did not like much, but he was not surprised by it either – especially if what Mike Burton had told him was true.

The blond man reached the top of the stairs and by the time Hunter, Amy and Simeon had caught him up, he was already across the hall, knocking on a wooden door. A man spoke in French and the blond man opened the door and went inside. A moment later, he reappeared and summoned the team forward.

'Monsieur Babineaux will see you now.'

Hunter smiled at the blond man. 'You're right about your friend by the way – he really likes a good joke.'

As the blond man scowled at him in confusion, Hunter stepped past him into the room and was joined by the others a moment later. The blond man closed the door behind him and left them in the room. It was a large, ornate study decorated in the same Baroque fashion as they had seen elsewhere on their little tour of the chateau, with dark wooden-panelled walls and oil paintings everywhere. Hunter also spied a substantial wall of books to their left, mostly leatherbound volumes and all looking very rare and expensive. He also took note of a black crystal chan-delier, although today the light was being supplied by two enor-mous arched windows about ten feet apart. In front of the windows was an expansive mahogany desk, covered in yet more books and papers and an antique globe. Behind the desk was a leather swivel chair facing away from them, to be able to look through either one of the two windows.

Hunter could see Babineaux was clearly sitting in the chair and, for whatever reason, making them stew. Then without turning around, he spoke to them, which Hunter found vaguely comical, being able to see only the very top of the man's head – a luxurious silver bouffant – shining dully in the light coming through the window and hearing his deep French accent.

'Why have you come to my chateau, *hein*? I ask myself why are there three people standing in my study today, one of whom is holding a piece of my merchandise?'

'Because we have some questions to ask you about it,' Amy said tartly, surprising Hunter.

'I do not usually answer questions,' the cold voice said. 'Especially when they are asked by total strangers.'

'But I think you should answer my question today,' Amy said.

A pause. 'And why might that be?'

'Because I have many high connections in the FBI and CIA, and I've already told them about my visit here today.'

She was lying. Hunter knew that, but it was a clever gambit. The part about having contacts in the FBI and CIA was true enough, but she had told no one about their visit today to the chateau. Perhaps, Hunter considered somewhat grimly, that might have been a good idea. But he had faith in Amy's ability to bluff Babineaux and listened intently to the rest of the conversation.

'You are threatening me?' Babineaux said coolly.

'No. I'm only pointing out I'm not just any old stranger. The US is a powerful country, and the CIA especially has a very long reach. If anything happens to us here today, there are senior people in that organisation who will make you pay for it in ways you don't want to consider.'

Hunter was impressed by Amy's bluster, the sheer bravado it had taken to talk to this man in this way, but it didn't seem to have the same impact on Babineaux, who was now chuckling in his chair. He finally decided to swivel around and face them, revealing a very lean, very tanned man with slightly gaunt cheeks, freshly shaven and smelling of luxurious aftershave. He was wearing what was clearly an expensive hand-tailored suit, single-breasted style with a crisp white shirt and a conservative red maroon tie. His eyes were bright and keen and yet shadowed slightly by something Hunter could only think of as his evil past.

'You think I'm frightened of the CIA?'

'I think you should be,' Amy said. 'Look, all we want is a couple of questions answered and we can be on our way.'

'Are you some kind of private investigator?'

'You could say that,' Hunter said, stepping into the conversation. 'Our business does not directly involve you, Monsieur Babineaux. One of our teammates and several of our friends – including a senior FBI agent – were kidnapped recently by a strange religious organisation who think of themselves as some kind of Illuminati. They are holding them in exchange for a religious artefact in our possession which they want very badly. None of this has anything to do with you, but we think you may be able to lead us to these people.'

'How do you know I am not Illuminati?'

'Exactly!' Simeon said. 'He cannot be trusted.'

'We don't know if you're Illuminati,' Amy said. 'But I don't think you are. I think you're a businessman, not some religious kook concerned about what happened thousands of years ago.'

The man laughed again, but colder.

'Where is this religious artefact?'

'That's not important,' Hunter said, thinking about Blanco and Jodie outside the chateau.

'It might be important to me,' Babineaux said. 'Maybe I like religious artefacts.'

'We need to know about your business activities with the Zlobin weapons manufacturer,' Hunter said, reaching into his pocket and pulling out the detonator. 'This, I believe, is one of yours.'

Hunter slid the detonator across the desk until Babineaux was able to reach it. He picked it up and held it to the light of the windows behind him. He turned it a few times in his hand, nodded then set it back down on the desk and pushed it back across the desk to Hunter.

'Yes, this is one of mine. I have a special arrangement with Zlobin Industries and they supply me with a range of equipment that I can sell to interested parties.'

'The people that kidnapped our friends are one of those interested parties,' Amy said. 'We want to know where we can find them.'

'Well, that makes two of us,' Babineaux said.

Hunter and Amy glanced at one another. Hunter said, 'I don't understand – what do you mean by that?'

'I mean that these people who bought the explosives from me a few months ago have not yet paid fully for them. They owe me a lot of money. They called themselves a religious extremist group and when my people looked into them, the name Illuminati came up. Of course, I dismissed that as nonsense, but now you have my interest.'

'Can you tell us anything about these people?' Amy asked. 'You must have some kind of information on them to help us trace them?'

Monsieur Babineaux sighed and rose from his chair, slipped one hand in his suit jacket pocket and strolled over to the window. 'I've always been fascinated by mazes. I loved them as a child. People think I was born in a rough, inner-city suburb and raised on the streets, but this is not true. I was born into money just like my father and grandfather before me. How do you say in English – with the silver spoon in the mouth? As a child, I played in the mazes in my father's mansion, not far southwest from here, just around the other side of Paris. The thrill of the maze, getting lost, using your intelligence to find your way out. I always find my way out of mazes. I always find a solution to my problems. Sometimes through hard work, sometimes through pure thought, and sometimes serendipitous fate. In this case, I believe fate has brought you here.'

'What are you proposing?' Simeon asked. 'That we work together?'

'No, I don't work with other people. But I think that I will give you one of my men. You have already met him – he has very blond hair. His name is Volkov, and he is from Moscow. He is a very good man, brave and fights with courage. I think perhaps he can join you on your journey and help you get my money back. He likes jokes.'

'I'm not sure about that,' Amy said, shooting a glance at Hunter.

Babineaux shrugged. 'You take Volkov with you, or you'll never leave this room alive.'

'When you put it like that,' Hunter said, 'I think we could use all the help we can get.'

Amy backed down. Hunter could see she had no trouble believing Babineaux's threat. 'But have you got any leads on how we can find these people?'

'Not many – only the address of a middleman who acted as a kind of broker between the two parties. His name is Michel Dupont. You have to understand that I'm not in the habit of giving people millions of dollars of weapons without taking a certain amount of collateral upfront. In this case, they paid 25 per cent with a promise to pay the balance upon delivery, but when we delivered the weapons, they had assembled an enormous force of highly skilled fighters who killed my team and ran away with the weapons. This only happened a few weeks ago, and I am in the process of tracking them down so they can be brought here to the chateau and executed. And now all of a sudden you turn up. It seems that our friends in the Illuminati are happy to double-cross anyone they meet. I don't care about your religious artefact, I just want the men who robbed me on their knees in this study begging for their lives. Do we have a deal?'

'We cannot deal with this man!' Simeon said with a sense of real urgency in his voice. 'Everyone in France knows how shady he is! He will betray us at the first opportunity.'

Hunter heard everything Simeon was saying and a good part of him completely agreed, but he also knew that this meeting could have gone in a very different direction, which was why Amy had asked Blanco and Jodie to remain out of sight with the sword.

'I don't see that we really have much choice,' Hunter said.

'You do not have any choice,' Babineaux said. 'I am offering you an extra man for your team, and an open chequebook to hunt down these thieving bastards.'

'Then we have a deal,' Amy said. 'The first thing we need to know is, where is this middleman?'

'You cannot find Michel Dupont,' Babineaux said. 'He is very careful about this, but we have learnt that he likes to take drugs, illegal drugs. He buys them from a piece of junk called Pascal Dujardin. Now, him you can find, and he will lead you to Dupont.'

'All right,' Amy said. 'How do we find this drug dealer?'

Babineaux gave her a mischievous grin. 'Listen carefully.'

## 12

Saint-Denis to Paris's north was not an area of the city that tourists often found themselves in, and Hunter understood why when they stepped up out of the Mercedes and looked around. Everywhere he looked was a rundown apartment block covered in graffiti, and there were copious amounts of dog excrement on the pavements. He saw an upturned bin with litter spilling out of it, blowing all down the street, and somewhere in a different street, a car alarm was blaring.

'They should put this place on the postcards,' Blanco said, still hefting the backpack containing the sword.

'They still do postcards?' Hunter asked.

'Yeah, sure they do,' Jodie said. 'I saw some in a tourist shop somewhere along the way.'

'That's very reassuring to know,' Hunter said. 'One doesn't like to think of the entire world being transported onto the mysterious cloud.'

Amy frowned as she looked around. 'Whether it's in the cloud or on a postcard, this place ain't getting any attention anytime soon from the tourist industry.'

'Where exactly does this middleman live again?' Jodie asked.

'Just up here on the right,' Amy said.

'And when we get there,' Volkov said, 'I do talking.'

'Who made you the boss of us?' Simeon said. 'We don't do what you say just because you work for a man like Monsieur Babineaux!'

'Hang on a minute,' Hunter said, looking at Simeon. 'You've only been on the team, like, one hour longer than this guy. You're talking as if you've been with us from the very beginning.'

'You are lucky to have me on board!' Simeon said, tapping his temple with his finger. 'You should let me have more of a say – after all, I am the only French person on this team. Only I will be able to understand the psychology of this so-called middleman, this Pascal Dujardin.'

Hunter doubted that. Since joining the HARPA team all those years ago, he had dealt with dozens if not hundreds of criminals, gangsters, thieves, liars and psychopaths, and if anything was true of all of them, it was that they shared critical parts of their personality profile. They had no ethics, they had no moral compass. They didn't mind stealing from other people or hurting them, and they enjoyed taunting them. They felt they had a right to take whatever they pleased even if it had nothing to do with them. He doubted Dujardin was any different from any of the characters he had met, no matter how French he was. On the other hand, it was extremely useful that Simeon had joined the team, as he was the only properly fluent French speaker. Hunter's French was passable, but in certain situations, he knew nothing beat having a native command of a language.

They continued down the pavement, Hunter keenly avoiding the canine calling cards as much as he could before finally arriving in the lobby area of a ten-storey-high tenement block. The interior was dark and grimy and smelled faintly of the unsavoury activities of drunks. There were two lift doors in front of them, both covered in graffiti, and off to the left was the base of a stairwell leading up to the floors above.

'We should split up,' Volkov said. 'Some of us should go in elevator and some of us should use stairs. It's just how I like to do business. If they somehow think we come after them, they could escape. I don't like to leave them any opportunities to get away from me once the hunt has begun.'

Hunter shrugged. 'Sure, if you want to walk up ten flights of stairs, then you're more than welcome to do so.'

'I will also climb the stairs,' Simeon said.

'I'm definitely taking the elevator,' Blanco said. 'Don't forget this; it isn't just a sword in here, but half of our kit as well. I feel like a pack mule.'

'You'll be rewarded in heaven, Sal,' Jodie said. 'Definitely not before – not if I'm any judge of this world.'

'So cynical,' Volkov said, turning to face the young Californian. 'But such pretty face.'

Jodie gave him a suspicious glance and pushed the button for the lift. It arrived a few seconds later, and the doors creaked open and the team stepped inside. When they began to close, it was just in time to see Volkov and Simeon climbing up the stairs.

The team rode to the top floor in silence, and then the doors opened with a gentle ping to reveal a dark, damp corridor with threadbare carpet running off in both directions, each leading to various apartments.

'Which way is our place?' Jodie asked.

'Down here on the left,' Amy said. 'According to Volkov, he's in number 143.'

They waited for Volkov and Simeon to join them, then moved along the corridor until they were outside Dujardin's apartment. Everyone stayed out of sight of the spy hole apart from Jodie, who now knocked on the door and tried to look as young and innocent as possible. They heard a lock and chain being jiggled from the other side of the door and then the door swung open. Without waiting for an invitation, Hunter stepped into view, grabbed the man by the throat and pushed him back. At the same time, Blanco, Simeon, Jodie, Amy and Volkov hurried into the apartment. The Russian closed the door.

Hunter pushed Dujardin all the way through to the sitting room at the far end of the apartment and forced him down into a chair.

'*Qu'est-ce que c'est que ça?*' he asked.

'We ask the questions,' Hunter said.

'English?'

'We're looking for someone and you're going to help us find him,' Hunter said.

'Looking for who?' Dujardin said. He was in his early twenties and had a little bit of peach fuzz around his face. He was wearing a black beanie at an odd angle on his head and wore a hoodie with a picture of a surfboard on it, and baggy blue jeans. He had some trainers on his feet that looked about the same size as astronaut boots.

'You deal drugs to a man we need to talk to,' Hunter said. 'His name is Michel Dupont and no one seems to know where he lives.'

'*Vous êtes des flics?*' The man looked frantically at the sea of faces in his apartment. 'Are you cops?'

Hunter sighed. 'If you don't tell us where Dupont lives, you'll wish we were cops by the time we leave this apartment.'

'I don't need this kind of heat just because I might sell some merchandise to someone from time to time,' Dujardin said. 'Dupont has a large house overlooking the Seine. I'll give you his address. Tell him from me he is a piece of shit and I never want to sell to him again.'

'Tell him yourself,' Hunter said. 'But give me the address first.'

Dujardin reeled off the address, and then the team made their way back along the corridor and out into the lobby where they called up another lift. Volkov and Simeon decided the stairs were not necessary this time and the entire party stepped into the lift and went down to the ground floor together. They stepped out of the lift and walked back out into the grim rundown streets of Saint-Denis before making their way back to the Mercedes.

Arriving in central Paris, they drove along the north bank of the Seine, cruising in the watery sun on a wide two-lane boulevard separated by a row of trees, called the Quai de l'Hôtel de Ville. Then they reached the Pont Marie, an ancient cobblestone bridge arched in the usual style of Paris, before driving onto Île Saint-Louis, a small island just to the east of Île de la Cité, the island where Notre Dame was located. They now drove south on the Rue des Deux Ponts and then turned into the Rue Budé, the small side street where Dupont lived. It was a narrow road, only wide enough to accept one vehicle at a time, and the pavements were only a couple of feet wide. The road was almost entirely residential, although there were a handful of commercial properties such as cafés, a flower shop and also a shop selling small bespoke furniture. To Hunter, the prices looked high, but that was to be expected in an area like this. As they continued down the street, Hunter looked up to see only a narrow ribbon of sky above them, caused by the tall, five-storey buildings running along each side of the road.

'All right, this is it,' Amy said. 'This is where Michel Dupont spends his time when he's not buying cocaine from scumbags like Dujardin.'

They got out of the SUV and after the driver explained that

he would have to park the car on the south of the island due to the narrowness of the road they were on, they watched him pull away.

They approached the address, and this time Hunter rang the bell and a moment later the intercom crackled. A low and gravelly voice spoke, one with an inherent tone of arrogance that Hunter immediately disliked.

'We need to speak to Michel Dupont,' Hunter said in English.

'Who is speaking please?'

'A friend of Pascal Dujardin says he has some extra merchandise for you. Hurry up, I can't be here for long. We need to be discreet.'

The intercom went dead and Amy stared at Hunter. 'You think that's going to work?'

Hunter shrugged. 'No idea. I'm an ex-army officer and an archaeologist, not somebody who buys cocaine from street thugs. Don't know the etiquette.'

Then the door opened and he saw a tall, smartly dressed man in a black roll-neck with expensive shoes and a bright sparkling Rolex watch strapped to a thin, pale wrist.

Volkov pushed past Hunter and stormed into Dupont's hallway, grabbing him by the throat just as Hunter had done earlier with Dujardin and forcing him back until he crashed into the bottom of his staircase. Hunter and the rest of the team stepped inside the house as quietly and discreetly as possible and Blanco clicked the door shut behind them. The older American man was grateful to set his backpack down in the hallway, giving it a loving tap as if it were a Labrador. At the same time, Volkov was talking to Dupont in menacing tones.

'Tell us what we want to know.'

'Listen – I've paid up everything I owe Dujardin,' Dupont said.

'So you can just get the hell out of here and tell him I owe him nothing!'

'We're not here for that, you stupid little scumbag,' Volkov said in his heavily accented broken English. 'Who you think we are – common drug dealing scum? We here because you do business with somebody who owes us money.'

Dupont's face suddenly changed entirely. His calm and somewhat confused demeanour had now turned to outright terror, and the colour drained away from his face. Hunter saw this was the moment reality had dawned on him for the first time.

'Oh, my God! You are from...'

'Is right. Monsieur Babineaux sends greetings.' Volkov planted an enormous, heavy-duty punch in Dupont's stomach that caused him to double over on the stairs, gasping and wheezing and reaching out for the banister rails to keep himself from falling all the way down onto the hall floor. When he had finally finished gasping for breath, Volkov spoke again.

'My employer provided you with weapons, which you provided to a third party – a bunch of clowns who call themselves Illuminati. Unfortunately, the Illuminati have not made the final payment on the weapons we gave them. Now we wish to collect money and you are going to tell us where to find them.'

Dupont was still heaving breath into his lungs, Volkov's punch quietly impressing Hunter, who was still standing in the hall with the others, watching the Russian working on the middleman.

'I don't know much about them, I swear! No!' Sensing Volkov was about to deliver another gift from Monsieur Babineaux in his stomach, he quickly spoke again. 'But I still might be able to help you!'

'I thought you might,' Volkov said. 'We need address and we need it now.'

Dupont reached into his pocket, which Hunter and everyone else could see contained no weapon and nothing but a phone, and now pulled that phone out, still holding his left hand up in front of Volkov's face, fingers spread wide and showing his palm to keep the Russian at bay. Dupont now used his right thumb to navigate his way out of trouble, rapidly coming up with an address.

'Here,' he said at last, turning the phone so Volkov could see it. 'I did business with a man who did indeed claim to be Illuminati, and he called himself Gaspard Floquet.'

'As in Bistro Floquet?' Simeon asked, amazed.

'Yes.'

Volkov paused and looked back to Hunter. 'We have address.'

Simeon laughed. 'Yes, but this is a problem.'

'Why does it present a problem?' Hunter asked.

'Because Gaspard Floquet owns one of the most famous restaurants in Paris – the Bistro Floquet!'

'I don't understand why that's a problem,' Jodie said. 'All these Illuminati dudes always seem to own something important. They're all connected.'

Simeon shrugged. 'Maybe, maybe not. But I think it is a problem because the Bistro Floquet is situated halfway up the Eiffel Tower.'

**13**

The misfit team emerged from the Mercedes beside Bir-Hakeim Metro station and after a short walk arrived at the base of the Eiffel Tower. There were four large kiosks built into the base of it, and now the team moved to the one on the southeast corner and booked the tickets required to go up to the restaurant on the second floor.

They split in two. Amy stayed on the ground guarding the sword and Jodie and Simeon were also on the ground, watching the tower's pillars in case Floquet managed to escape. Hunter, Volkov and Blanco decided not to use the south pillar staircase, where a daunting 674 steps awaited them. Instead, they took one of the lifts on the tower's east pillar which took them quickly up to the second floor. When the doors opened, they stepped out and Hunter was immediately impressed with the view stretching out across Paris. Years ago, he had taken the lift all the way to the summit of the tower with his French girlfriend Avril, and it was so high at 900 feet, it had been a somewhat hair-raising experience, especially as it was on a cold and windy February day. From that altitude, Paris seemed like a little toy town so far below, but from down here on the second floor, 377 feet above the ground, he was able to make out much finer detail, including people walking around on the beautiful gravel walkways in the park, and cars shuffling their way slowly through the traffic.

Turning to look inside the second floor, they quickly saw the Bistro Floquet and stepped inside. It was a large open-plan eating area, with glass walls and a glass roof, through which he looked up and followed the long stretch of the Eiffel Tower's iron neck stretching right up to the summit where he had been all those years before. Looking back now to Earth, or at least the second floor, he scanned the busy restaurant for any sign of Gaspard Floquet, whose ugly mug they had been shown by Amy on her telephone on their way across the city.

'Anyone see him yet?' Volkov asked. 'I can't see anyone who looks like picture Amy showed us.'

'All I see is waiters,' Blanco said.

Hunter was still scanning the busy restaurant. 'All I see is trouble.'

'And food,' Blanco said. 'All I see now is food.' Blanco was staring at the beautiful white linen tables and shining silver cutlery. 'This place is like paradise.' He stopped talking and paused to pick up a menu from an empty table beside him. 'Asparagus puff pastry, rouge Dauphine ravioli, duck pâté, ravioli stuffed with langoustine, French duck foie gras with Sarawak pepper; these look great, although I think I'll leave the rouge Burgundy snails for another time.'

'I think we'll leave all of it for another time,' Hunter said, pointing in the direction of the kitchens. 'I think I just caught a glimpse of Floquet. Am I right or am I right?'

Hunter had been mildly and briefly captivated by the menu in the same way as Blanco, particularly the roasted salmon steak and the Normandy beef tenderloin, between which he was having some difficulty making a choice. This was not a problem for the dessert course as they had a bourbon vanilla crème brulé at an absolute bargain of just fifteen euros. Then he had looked towards the kitchen just in time to see the face of Gaspard Floquet as he broke off a conversation with the Maître d' and then turned and stepped back into the kitchen.

'Is definitely him,' Volkov said. 'Let's go.'

Hunter almost moved to restrain the Russian but thought better of it. Floquet was the man they were looking for and there were very few places he could evade them up here on the second floor of the Eiffel Tower, and the ground was covered by the rest of the team. That left Volkov and Blanco to capture Floquet and get the information they needed out of him, with as little fuss as possible. Then either Floquet or his superior in the Illuminati would hopefully be able to lead them to wherever their friends were being kept hostage.

Hunter leaned into Blanco. 'Sal, you stay out here and make sure he can't get out this way.'

'No problem at all,' Blanco said. 'I don't suppose you guys mind if I order some wine and some of the strawberry cream cake while I'm waiting?'

Hunter smiled at him, knowing he was joking – or at least hoping he was, and went with Volkov. As they approached the bar area, behind which was a door to the kitchen, the waiter behind the cash register looked up at them and gave them a serious French smile before asking what they wanted to drink.

Volkov now surprised Hunter by pulling a Sig Sauer handgun from a shoulder holster under his suit and pushed past the barman without a word. Hunter had not stopped to consider if he was armed or not, but now he knew. Now, Hunter gave the barman an apologetic look and a shrug and followed Volkov through into the kitchen.

The world changed from one of peace and serenity to one of clattering pans and steaming pots, and chefs and sous chefs shouting at each other. There was the sound of laughter coming from someone to Hunter's left who was chopping some celery. A man whom Hunter presumed was the head chef caught sight of them and walked over. He was a walking cliché, weighing in at twenty stones and dressed in chef's whites. He was holding, somewhat disconcertingly, an extremely long and sharp-looking boning knife.

'Zere are no customers in ze kitchen,' he said without preamble. 'Please to be leaving.'

Volkov had been holding the gun behind his back as he approached the head chef, and now he brought it around and pointed it right in the middle of his face. The chef was focusing intently on the handgun that Volkov was pressing between his eyes. Involuntarily, he dropped the boning knife on the floor and it clattered on the tiles. He also raised his hands high in the air. Everyone in the kitchen immediately stopped work and stood staring in horror at what was unfolding in the heart of their world. The only sound was the gentle murmur of the crowd dining outside in the restaurant, and the bubble and hiss of pots and pans all around them.

'Where is Gaspard Floquet?' Volkov said quietly and calmly.

To his credit, the chef retained his dignity, stayed calm and simply pointed to the back of the kitchen where there was a door with a small round window in it. 'His office is through zere.'

'You have been very kind,' Volkov said, and then snapped the gun away from the man's forehead and made his way to the door.

Hunter gave the head chef another apologetic look and shrugged. 'He's very impatient. I'm so sorry.'

As Hunter followed Volkov to the office, he noticed movement inside through the small round window. He saw someone's head darting back and forth for a moment and then he was out of sight.

'Take it easy, Volkov,' Hunter said. 'I think we've been rumbled.'

'What is "rumbled"?'

The door with the window burst open to reveal Gaspard Floquet standing in front of them with a handgun. It was raised into the aim although not very professionally, and held with only one hand. He opened fire on the two men, without asking questions, almost hitting Volkov, who dived behind a row of steel kitchen cabinets. The rounds got nowhere near Hunter, who had been standing behind the Russian and who now rolled behind one of the islands in the kitchen. All the staff ran screaming from the kitchen and Hunter heard a roar of terror outside in the restaurant and the sound of dozens of chairs scraping on the floor as all the customers fled for their lives.

He clambered immediately up to his hands and knees as he tried to peer over the surface of the island and see where Floquet was. Completely unarmed, Hunter now raised his hand onto the island and fumbled around till he found a knife, pulling a twelve-inch carving knife off the side and gripping it in his right hand. On the other side of the kitchen, he heard Volkov firing his gun in the direction of Floquet, who now, unable to see either of the men who were attacking him, burst back through his office door and disappeared out of sight.

'We have to get after him!' Volkov said.

Hunter looked over the island and saw Volkov was already on his feet and charging towards Floquet's office door. Still armed with only the carving knife, Hunter now joined the Russian and the two men burst through the door just in time to see another door on the far side of the office – a fire exit of some kind – slowly closing.

'He's trying to get down to the ground!' Volkov said.

'He won't get much luck down there,' Hunter said, pulling out his phone. 'Because Amy, Jodie and Simeon are down there guarding the three elevator pillars. I'll call Amy and let her know what's going on.'

Blanco now burst through the door. Hunter saw he had also armed himself with a steak knife snatched from one of the tables.

'Heard some shots!' he said.

Volkov glanced at him. 'Good of you to join us.'

The three men ran to the fire door just in time to see Floquet, not racing down the steps towards the ground but racing up the steps towards the summit.

'What the hell is he doing?' Volkov asked.

'He presumes we've got people down on the ground and he's trying to buy time,' Hunter said. 'I guess he's going to call up some backup to help him out. I know I would, so this place is going to be crawling with Illuminati goons anytime now. It won't be him that's trapped up the top by us, but it'll be us that's trapped up the top by them! We have to get up there and get the information out of him as soon as possible. Sal, you stay on the second floor and stop anyone else coming up after us. Volkov, let's go!'

## 14

Hunter was in the lead now, with Volkov a few steps behind him. Carrying only a steak knife, he pounded up the metal steps to the summit. On the drive over, Amy had told him that there were 674 steps to the second floor, which were open to the public. There were another 991 steps from the second floor all the way to the summit, although the public were not allowed to use these steps after the second floor and were restricted to the lifts. Gaspard Floquet had been unable to reach the lifts due to his fleeing via the fire escape, so had now broken through the sign saying 'no public access' and was sprinting up the steps to the summit.

Hunter was still right behind him, but now Floquet turned and fired on him, causing him to slam his body up against the metal ironwork behind him. The bullet missed, ricocheting off a step and throwing off a shower of sparks, but Floquet didn't hang around to watch it. He was already on the move again, turning round on the landing and heading up the next flight of steps.

'Let me go in front!' Volkov shouted. 'I have gun, I can't get shot off with you in way!'

'Then give me the gun!' Hunter said.

Volkov looked at him with barely concealed contempt, pushed past him and pounded up the steps. He reached the landing in three strides, spun around and headed up the next flight running in the opposite direction. Hunter could see Volkov needed to work on his personality skills, and armed still only with his steak knife and a strong desire to have a firearm instead, he now ran up the steps behind the Russian. There was a strong cold wind blowing through the ironwork of the Eiffel Tower, and it cut right through Hunter as he continued to pursue Floquet, wondering how far he'd get and what would happen if he made the top. He paused for a moment to look down at the ground. There was no sign of Simeon or Jodie, but he could see Amy thanks to Blanco's bright red backpack, standing out away from the tower where they had agreed. Turning and carrying on up the steps, Hunter pulled his phone out and made a call to Amy.

'Amy, it's me! Floquet is trying to get to the summit of the tower. He must have worked out we have people on the ground and didn't want to risk his chances down there until backup arrived.'

'I can see you now, Max,' Amy said. 'You're running up the outer steps on the way up to the summit, is that right?'

'Yeah, that's me. How far above me are Floquet and Volkov?'

'Floquet is about five or six flights above you, and Volkov's in between the two of you. You should be careful up there – is there any way you can fall?'

'Amy, we have to make sure we get hold of Floquet before the backup arrives. I'm not going to just suddenly tumble off the steps and fly down to the ground. Relax.'

'You won't be flying, believe me.'

'Listen. I've got an idea. I think we're going to need Floquet's Illuminati backup to be tied up in problems down there rather than just divert up here. If they do get into the tower then Blanco is on the second floor, but he won't be able to hold them back for long.'

'Suggestions?'

'I know this is the nuclear option, but I think that you should call the police and tell them there's a terror threat in the Eiffel Tower. Just improvise, I don't care. You can use the scene back at the restaurant to help you out.'

'Scene?'

'Floquet fired on us and caused total mayhem. There are dozens of terrified diners heading your way. Use that. Get the cops here. They'll be there in minutes and then that's going to make it much harder for any Illuminati backup to get inside the tower.'

'But what about you?' Amy asked.

'Believe me, if there's a terror threat, there's not going to be a problem getting out of this tower. As soon as word gets out, they'll begin evacuation proceedings, and then everyone will be cleared from the tower. Providing we've already got the information we need out of Floquet, we can just stream out with everybody else and then we can get on and get Quinn.'

'That sounds like a great idea,' Amy said. 'I'll give the police a call right now and tip them off. In the meantime, just take care of yourself.'

'That has been my plan from the very beginning,' Hunter said.

Hunter cut the call and continued his way up the steps. He heard gunfire exchanged between Floquet and Volkov, but then two sets of footsteps told him no one had hit their mark. He knew from long experience that it wasn't as easy as the movies made it look, to hit a moving target, especially one that definitely did not want to be hit. He began to catch up to Volkov, but as he turned around on the landing to take the next flight up, he just caught sight of the Russian's jacket flapping out of view.

He raced up to the flight of steps in front of him and when he turned onto the next landing, he was surprised to see he'd made it to the top. He recognised it at once from his visit all those years ago – it always seemed to be much further to the ground from up here. The actual summit level of the Eiffel Tower was built around a central office, reconstructed to look like the one used by Gustav Eiffel. Running around the outside was a viewing walkway, protecting people from accidental falls or deliberate jumps by a sturdy metal cage. Seeing neither Volkov nor Floquet anywhere in sight, Hunter, still gripping his steak knife, decided to make his way around the platform, but then he heard gunshots coming from the opposite direction he had chosen and spun around, making his way to the first corner. When he turned, he saw Floquet on the floor clutching his stomach, blood pumping out and staining his white shirt dark red. Volkov was standing above him, his gun in his right hand. Hunter saw Floquet's handgun several yards away, clearly having been kicked out of reach by Volkov.

'What happened?' Hunter asked.

The Russian shrugged. 'We fired at each other, but it turns out I am better shot. Now he bleeds to death on summit of Eiffel Tower.'

Floquet was panicking. Hunter saw sweat beading on his forehead and his hands were trembling. He had been shot more than once, and blood was pumping quickly from his torso. Hunter knew survival from multiple gunshot wounds to the stomach was not the most likely outcome awaiting Gaspard Floquet. While he had little sympathy for a man who was involved in illegal weapons trafficking and quite possibly had helped orchestrate the kidnapping of Quinn Mosley and his other friends, he did care about finding Quinn, and this man right now was their only lead. He pushed past Volkov and squatted down until he was eye to eye with Floquet.

'I need you to tell me something, Floquet,' Hunter began. 'We know that you were in charge of the transfer of weapons from Monsieur Babineaux to the Illuminati unit that packed explosives inside a warehouse in London. We also know that you have not paid Mr Babineaux for most of the weapons and he's not very happy about it.'

'He has paid,' Volkov said. 'He has paid with his life.'

Floquet's eyes darted from the Russian back to Hunter, and as Hunter had hoped, in his dying moments he saw Hunter as the good cop.

'That is correct,' Floquet said weakly. 'I was in charge of the deal. But it was not my decision to rip off Monsieur Babineaux. I was told to do so by my Illuminati superior.'

'Interesting you should mention that,' Hunter said. 'You see, I'm looking for some friends the Illuminati kidnapped, and I know that it was organised by the man at the very top – he calls himself Oriax, but obviously that's not his real name. I need to find Oriax and right now you're my only lead. Is he your superior? How do I find him?'

'You honestly think I'm going to tell you that?' Floquet began to smile serenely as he looked up at the clouds. Hunter saw he was fading out.

'You'll tell me one way or the other,' Hunter said. As he spoke, he lifted Floquet's lapel and searched his jacket for a telephone. He found a smartphone inside his pocket and tried to open it but was blocked by the key code security screen.

'Do you have Illuminati contacts on here?' Hunter asked.

Floquet coughed blood. 'Of course not, I'm no fool.'

Hunter sighed, not because he didn't believe him but because he did.

'Volkov – can you get a section of this security mesh off?'

The Russian looked at the special security screen that was put up to stop people from falling off the top of the tower. He examined it for a few moments and then gave a curt decisive nod. 'Yes. Is easy.'

'How long will it take?'

'Not long,' Volkov said, touching one of the nuts and bolts that held the panel of mesh in place. He aimed his handgun, turned his head away and fired, blowing one of the nuts and bolts to pieces. 'It will take three times longer than that.'

'Do it,' Hunter said. 'We haven't got long – the police are going to be here any minute and then we lose our last chance.'

'Why?' Volkov asked. 'We can't get down, even if we can go over the outside through the mesh.'

'We're not going anywhere,' Hunter said. 'But Monsieur Floquet here is going to be the first restauranteur to fly off the Eiffel Tower.'

A look of horror appeared on Floquet's face. The look of serenity Hunter had noticed earlier was because the Frenchman knew he was dying and that it would be a simple matter of waiting until his blood pressure dropped and then he would pass out and die in peace. What the Englishman was now proposing was an entirely different end. Several seconds of abject terror followed by a brutal and final impact on concrete, and that was presuming he didn't catch on one of the iron girders on the way down and ended up spinning and crashing and banging into various parts of the tower before meeting his end.

As Volkov fired his gun and blasted off the second bolt securing the mesh panel in place, Floquet's eyes widened with horror and he waved his right hand in the air. 'Stop! Please stop!

I'll tell you what you want. Just let me die here in peace, please. I beg of you!'

'Get talking,' Hunter said. Far below, the streets of Paris were echoing with the sound of dozens of emergency services sirens, all in response to Amy's telephone call alerting them about the terror attack at the tower.

'I was ordered not to pay Monsieur Babineaux by my superior in the Illuminati. His name is Werner Nachtnebel. He owns a nightclub in Berlin called Spionage. You will find him there.'

'What does he look like, this Nachtnebel?' Hunter said.

'You can't miss him. He is very tall and he has pure white hair. He likes to be in the club when it's open. He enjoys seeing his empire in all its glory. He likes the women, too. He will lead you to Oriax.'

'You think he tells truth?' Volkov asked. 'Because I really want to throw him off tower.'

'He's telling the truth,' Hunter said. 'I can tell by the look in his eyes.'

But now there was nothing in his eyes because Gaspard Floquet was dead.

Hunter didn't care much; he had the information he was looking for and now he had to get down to the second floor as quickly as possible and then play the part of a terrified tourist being shepherded out of the Eiffel Tower. Then when the team had gathered together out on the Champs de Mars, they could share the information they had and plan the next part of their journey.

Volkov looked at him. 'I can at least throw body off tower?'

'What is wrong with you, Volkov?' Hunter asked.

The Russian shrugged and the two men made their way back down to Blanco on the second floor. Hunter was absolutely sure he could save Quinn's life now, but first, they had a quick stop to make in the French Alps.

## 15

Quinn Mosley was surprised to hear the voices of Jim Gates and his wife and Professor Juliette Bonnaire when she woke from her drug-induced slumber on board what appeared to be yet another aircraft. Since her kidnapping, she had been kept apart from the other hostages, but for some reason now they had decided to put them all together in the same space. She was grateful for that and was pleased finally to be able to talk to somebody she trusted. Unfortunately, thanks to the hood she was being forced to wear, she couldn't see them.

'Jim, hey.'

'Is that you, Quinn?'

'Yeah, it's me. I wish I could see you.'

'Me too. You're hooded too, huh?'

'Yeah. I seem to have spent most of the last day or so with a hood on my head and these guys also seem to enjoy pumping me full of drugs.'

'Yeah, we got that too,' Gates said.

'Are we alone?' Quinn asked.

'Yes,' Gates replied. 'I've been listening out for them for a long time. There's no way anyone could be that silent for so long.'

Quinn heard rustling now and guessed Jim and Susanna Gates were sitting beside one another, their hands cuffed behind their backs, just like hers.

'It's good to hear some other voices,' Juliette said. 'I've been kept on my own since they kidnapped me from my Paris apartment. Who are these people?'

'One of them spoke to me,' Quinn said. 'He spoke to me a few times. He said they're Illuminati, but I think they understand this to mean something different than we do. I think they're some sort of religious extremists.'

'You think this man was lying to you?' Juliette said.

'No, I don't think so, Professor,' Quinn said. 'I trust Jophiel; at least, I trust him to give me information. I wouldn't trust him with my life, although I might have to...'

'What do you mean by that?' Gates asked.

Quinn felt a wave of fear flow through her. 'Haven't they told you why we're here yet?'

'No one has spoken to us since they kidnapped us from our home,' Susanna Gates said.

Quinn could hear she had been crying, and sympathised. Her involvement with a business like this would always have been indirect, through her husband Jim. Gates was a man of few words, and he might have shielded his wife from the activities of HARPA and his professional life throughout his career. She guessed that Susanna Gates was the weak link in the chain, as far as this small group of hostages was concerned.

'Jophiel told me HARPA found Excalibur, or what turned out to be the Sword of the Archangel Michael, in Cornwall. They actually found it. As soon as the Illuminati found out they discovered it, they wanted to make a trade – our lives for the sword.'

'Why didn't they just take the sword back to Cornwall?' Juliette said.

'I don't know,' Quinn said. 'But knowing HARPA, I expect they fought and destroyed whatever enemy they were fighting there and the Illuminati decided to take another course, and an altogether more subtle one.'

'Kidnapping us and trading our lives for the sword,' Gates said with disgust.

'That's about the size of it,' Quinn said.

'They'll never do it,' Gates said. 'I know Amy Fox better than anyone and there's no way she will hand over an ancient relic of that degree of importance, particularly a biblical relic, to a bunch of terrorists. I don't care if they call themselves the Illuminati or not, that's all they are – terrorist scum. They traumatised my wife, and they'll pay for that with their lives.'

Quinn heard Susanna Gates gasp when she heard her husband speaking like this.

'And I know Max Hunter better than anyone else,' Juliette said. 'He will not risk the lives of friends or colleagues under any circumstances. I think he would care much more about our lives than a relic. There may be an argument between Max and Amy. If what you say is true, Mr Gates, perhaps Amy is arguing never to return the sword, but Max is arguing to return it and trade it for our lives!'

Quinn said, 'There's no way they're going to give the Illuminati the Sword of Archangel Michael. I think they'll all agree on that, but I think they'll also all agree that they have to save our lives.'

The cabin fell silent, and Quinn felt another wave of fear, this time stained with nausea, at the predicament she and her friends were in. Amy would not let her die, but exactly how much of this situation Amy was controlling... she had no idea. Quinn guessed not much. Inside her hooded world, she closed her eyes and began to pray to a god she had never really believed in.

## 16

Flying in a Diamond DA62 rented by the Guild of St. Michael, they approached Courchevel from the north, navigating the aircraft carefully around the western slopes of the Bellecôte mountain, a large peak on the Vanoise massif. The evening light was weak and thin at this time of year and colouring the slopes a soft, coral pink. From up here, the pistes and ski runs were visible all over the slopes, meandering like frozen rivers across a fairytale landscape. Simeon was flying the aircraft, another skill he had kept to himself until the last possible moment, and was now cutting down into a narrow valley before beginning the notorious final approach into Courchevel Altiport.

'I hope we make it.'

On hearing Jodie's voice, Hunter turned in his seat to face her. The young Californian was gazing dreamily through her window, watching the mountainsides slowly rising up to meet them as they made their descent. She had uttered the words so quietly, he thought they were meant only for her and wondered whether he should reply or not.

'Depends where Simeon got his pilot's licence,' he said.

'I meant the mission,' Jodie said. 'Not the flight.'

'Montpellier Flight Academy,' Simeon said through the comms. 'One of the best flight schools in France. Just thought I'd throw that in.'

'We'll make it,' Blanco said. 'Just you see.'

Jodie twisted in her seat to reply to Blanco. 'I wish I could be as sure as you, Sal.'

'You're not normally this doubtful,' Amy said. 'Is everything all right?'

Jodie shrugged. 'Sure, but it's just something about this mission that's getting to me. Maybe it's because those crazies are holding so many of our friends hostage, or maybe it's the idea of Oriax getting his hands on the sword and...'

'And abusing its powers to fulfil this so-called prophecy?' Amy said.

'Prophecy.' Volkov huffed out a cynical laugh. 'Is nonsense.'

'But what if it's not?' Jodie countered.

'Is,' Volkov said.

Amy glared at him. 'It might help if we knew more precisely what the prophecy was, before we decide if it's nonsense or not.'

'Thanks to Simeon, we know enough,' Hunter said. 'The Guild of St Michael have always believed that whoever wields the sword will be as powerful as a god.'

'Not as a god, but as God,' Simeon said, defiantly. 'There is a distinction.'

'Quite,' Hunter put in. 'No harm meant, Simeon. Spending so much time studying ancient civilisations that generally practised polytheism, these things just slip out.'

'No problem,' Simeon said. 'And something tells me when we rescue Professor Toussaint from these madmen, he will finally accept it is time to tell me – to tell all of us – the full prophecy, the one handed down to him by the Guild across the centuries.'

'You think Oriax knows the full prophecy?' Jodie asked.

'Yes,' Amy replied with conviction. 'I think with Oriax we're dealing with a man who has spent years in the dark, researching, learning everything there is to know about the sword. He finally acted only when everything was in place and he was sure of success. He kidnapped federal agents, remember. That alone is twenty years to life.'

'The least of his crimes,' Volkov said gruffly. 'He is also violent killer with the blood of many innocent and not so innocent lives on his hands.'

'I think he knows about the prophecy too,' Simeon said. 'More than I know, for sure.'

'Why did Professor Toussaint never tell you the full truth? Surely you deserve to know,' Hunter asked.

Simeon smiled. 'As I mentioned before, in the Guild, there has always been a strict rule that only the mentor may know the full truth. We all know this when we join and we must accept it. However, the situation is now so dire I believe Professor Toussaint will share the truth. Then we will at last know the full story.'

Blanco shifted awkwardly in the cramped seat. 'I'm not sure I want to know any more than I already do.'

'I hear that, man,' Jodie said, turning to face the front.

'Everyone, prepare for landing,' Simeon said. 'This could get a little rough.'

'Freeing the professor or the landing?' Jodie asked.

'Both, I guess,' Simeon said, and he fell silent as his concentration grew. Speed reduced, flaps out and gear down. Hands gripping the yoke as he carefully steered the plane past the forested slopes of a mountain dangerously close to his port wing. Ahead, over the Bozel Valley, he saw the infamous runway. Built into the mountain with a gradient slope of nearly 20 per cent, the runway was considered one of the most dangerous in Europe. There were no instrument approach procedures and no runway lighting. But what really troubled Simeon was its short length and lack of a go-around procedure.

Most runways gave pilots the option of aborting the landing and going around to try again, but not Courchevel. Here, any hope of a go-around was destroyed by the massive mountain slopes rising at the end of the runway. Landing was tricky at the best of times, but approaching a runway with a mountain at the end of it was an altogether different problem. Foggy weather and other low visibility use of the airport was a strict no-no.

'We will soon break Professor Toussaint out of the Illuminati safe house they are holding him in,' Simeon said, casting his eye one more time over the instruments. 'God willing.'

Simeon reduced speed again and brought the plane level with the runway. Low enough so the treetops of the forest in front of the runway were nearly scraping the bottom of the plane. He remembered the words of an old pilot friend of his who had ferried skiers here for many years: get the thing down right at the very start of the tarmac. The 'thing' was the plane.

Simeon blew out a breath. 'I've done it at other airports, I can do it here. I hope.'

Amy gawped at him. 'You hope?'

He said nothing but then the plane was down. A little heavier than he would have liked, but not bad enough to put a dent in the Guild's insurance policy. He pulled the throttles back and slammed the engine into reverse, bringing the small turboprop to a juddering, whining stop, and then increased speed a little to taxi the rest of the way up the sloping runway to the parking area at the top.

'Sorry about the landing,' Simeon said, driving over to the tiny Altiport.

'Good work, Siméon,' Hunter said. 'We're all down safe. That's what counts.'

They disembarked and wandered into the small building. They showed their passports, and a woman behind the desk greeted them with a smile and processed their paperwork.

'*Bienvenue à Courchevel*,' she said as she handed their passports back. 'Welcome to Courchevel.'

When they stepped back out in the crisp mountain air, Simeon's phone rang. It was a call from a local Guild Chapter he had organised as a backup. They were ready and in place and waiting for his orders. 'There are not many of them and they are not well armed, as I have explained, but it is better than nothing. I must take this call.'

'*Allô*, Boucher. All good?' he asked.

'So far,' came the reply.

'And what about the mentor? Is he safe?'

'Alive and kicking, for now. Why not come over and have a look for yourself?'

'Good idea. With you in ten.'

The drive into the ski resort was short and easy and offered stunning views north across the beautiful Tarentaise Valley. On the far side of the valley was the Bellecôte mountain they had just flown over in their turboprop. If anything, it looked even more impressive from here than from above.

They navigated smooth, bending roads lined with some of the most luxurious ski chalets in the world. Life here was quiet today. A man in overalls was unloading boxes of flowers from the back of a blue Citroen van and walking them over to a boutique. Further ahead, two older men were smoking and arguing, oblivious to the world around them. Beyond them, a young family was unpacking their belongings outside the front of a hotel ahead of a week's holiday, their children laughing and playing in the soft alpine light.

Amy looked on jealously. 'I always wanted to vacation here,' she said, almost to herself.

'Who can blame you?' Blanco said. 'It's breathtaking.'

Amy laughed. 'And yet the first time I finally get around to being here, it's on a case to rescue a kidnapped man. Not exactly the break I had in mind.'

They rounded a tight hairpin bend, sloping up towards the west end of the resort. Thick tranches of fir trees separated even more expensive chalets and cabins as they drove past an impressive hotel, built mostly from wood and designed in the traditional French style. Passing through a wooden gatehouse, they drove down an unsealed gravel track and finally reached their destination, an area just down the road from the Illuminati safe house that gave them a good view of it while obscuring them behind trees. They parked up behind the Guild's SUV and climbed out of their vehicle, wandering over to join them.

'I see you brought some friends, Simeon,' he said.

'They can be trusted, brother,' Simeon said, making some fast introductions. 'This is the HARPA team, or some of it. Like us, they had some of their own taken from them by Oriax and his men. Max, Amy, Sal, Jodie... this is Jules Droz, the local leader. He's a tough ex-cop from Marseille who joined the Guild many years ago. He has weapons.'

Hunter shook his hand. Droz was wearing a black beanie over his head to keep out the cold, and a faded camo jacket. Leaning on the car beside him was another Guild member, a large man in a thick black Parka.

'And this is Henri Lacroix, his number two.'

'Good to meet you both,' Amy said.

'How are things here?' Simeon asked Droz.

'All quiet,' Droz said in a raspy voice. 'The mentor has been in the property since we arrived. We presume he has been here since they snatched him in Montpellier. There are around half a dozen Illuminati men in there, led by a man named Sorin Goga, a Romanian who has worked with Oriax for many years. None of them has left the house since we arrived. Actually, Goga seems to lead a very boring existence. He reads, he makes coffee. Occasionally, he really shakes things up and looks out of a window. But never at us. I feel heartbroken.'

Lacroix opened a flask of coffee and poured it into some cups he had arranged on the SUV's roof. 'Here, Jules. Take a drink of this. It might cheer you up.'

'Thanks.'

Droz took the cup and drank some coffee, exaggeratedly smacking his lips before winking at Amy and handing her his binoculars. They had a clear enough view of the place through the trees with their binoculars, but Goga and his men, plus Toussaint, would be largely unaware of them. Just the way Droz wanted it.

Amy scanned the house. 'Where are they now?'

'On the second floor,' Lacroix said. 'That's where his main living area is. The lower floor is a garage and woodshed.'

Amy pushed the binoculars up and found Toussaint. He was in his fifties, a little tubby with a few strands of grey hair but mostly bald. Red cheeks and a peaceful expression on his face. She could just make out a mantelpiece and a fire, which was lit and roaring away.

'Yes, very nice,' she said. 'Very cosy. Especially compared to standing out here freezing our asses off.'

'The glamour of rescue and retrieval work,' Jodie said, taking one of the three cups Lacroix had prepared for his own team. 'Thanks, Henri. This is most welcome.'

'That was mine, but sure...' he said with a smirk. 'I can see you're a lady not to be argued with.'

'An astute observation, my new French friend,' Jodie said.

'Don't worry,' Volkov said. 'Her bite is worse than her bark.'

Lacroix frowned. 'I'm not sure you got that right.'

'Oh, he got it right,' Hunter said, sipping more coffee.

Simeon was now using the binoculars. 'Wait, the Illuminati guard is getting up.'

He turned to Amy, who was also watching Toussaint through the window.

Droz looked like he was about to explode. 'You mean something is finally happening?'

Simeon handed Amy the binoculars. 'Maybe, let's just see what he does next. What do you think, Amy?'

Amy scanned the opulent property. 'I think it's very nice, but a little too close to both the road and the hotel over there, for me. Imagine having a cosy winter night interrupted by the annoying noises from guests or passing traffic.'

'I meant what do you think about the tactical situation,' Simeon said. 'Not the quality of the safe house!'

'But of course you did,' Jodie said. 'Check out the guard. He's now leaving the main room. He's going into the kitchen.'

'Is he on his own?' Amy asked.

'Hard to say, but from this angle, I'd say yes.' Jodie offered some chewing gum around. Only Hunter took some.

'I can't see anyone on the top floor,' Hunter said, slipping the stick of chewing gum into his mouth. 'In fact right now I can't see any of the Illuminati at all.'

Volkov commented, 'Is only one vehicle on drive.'

'There's a barn and a garage though,' Jodie said. 'Anyone else could have parked up and hidden a vehicle in either.'

'True,' Hunter said. 'But what's life without a few surprises?'

'Time for fast ingress,' Volkov said. 'Do it while the guard is out of room. In and out fast so he barely knows what's happening. That's my way.'

'Is that what the ladies say about you?' Jodie said, chuckling at her own joke.

'That's not kind,' Amy said.

Jodie contained herself. 'The truth seldom is.'

'We are not doing anything that will harm the mentor!' Simeon said.

'I agree, so let's get our minds back on the job,' said Hunter. 'Where is Goga now?'

'He's leaving the kitchen,' Jodie said. 'Going out of sight.'

Hunter waited patiently, still chewing. 'You guys like peppermint or spearmint?'

'Always peppermint,' Amy said.

'Freak,' said Jodie. 'Spearmint all the way.'

'I'm peppermint,' said Volkov.

Jodie laughed. 'Funny, I figure you as a Juicy Fruit sort of guy.'

'You know, you're about as funny as obituary column,' Volkov said. 'What you got, Hunter?'

Hunter's voice was quiet as he held the binoculars steady and waited for any sign of Goga appearing. 'Peppermint. Always peppermint. Goga is still not here. Anyone else got him?'

'A light just went on around the side of the house,' Droz said. 'That is the toilet.'

'How long do you think he'll be in there?' Lacroix asked.

Droz shrugged. 'Depends what he's doing in there, right?'

'I say we make a move while he's on the pot,' Hunter said. 'Agreed?'

A round of nods told Hunter it was time to move in and get Toussaint.

'Okay then, let's go and get our hands dirty,' he said. 'And make sure you keep Professor Toussaint out of your sights.'

Droz walked to the back of his van and swung open the doors. 'Everyone, tool up.'

## 17

Except for Blanco, whom Hunter and Amy had suggested stay back at the Guild's van with the sword, the teammates moved silently to the chalet, keeping inside a line of fir trees to stay out of sight. Courtesy of the Guild, they were armed with compact machine pistols, the weapon of choice for a mission involving close-quarter combat in enclosed environments such as the chalet. Hunter led the team up through the trees to the bottom of the house where they made their way round the back of the garage block, stepping momentarily into the view of a window on the west side of the chalet, which Hunter checked. Seeing it was clear of any Illuminati spies, he led the team forward to a covered parking area built into the side of the house. There was a wooden door at the end of this area, in front of which was a doormat, some walking boots and a large metal vase filled with some umbrellas, and on the wall were some hooks, with some hats and coats hanging from them. When everyone had gathered together in the covered area, all armed and ready to go, Hunter opened fire on the door and blasted it to pieces. Then he smashed his way through it and charged into the house.

He found himself standing in a utility room with a sink, a washing machine, a tumble dryer and several large piles of linen stacked up on shelves. Ahead he saw another door, painted white and closed. He moved forward, gesturing the rest of the team to follow him with a waving motion of his right hand before opening the white door and finding himself in a dark landing at the bottom of some stairs. Turning to his right and seeing a bedroom, he realised the chalet had been designed to allow the sleeping accommodation on the ground floor so the living accommodation was on the first floor, allowing the residents to enjoy a superior view overlooking the mountains beyond. Was Toussaint being held down here?

Before he could look, he heard boots smashing their way down the stairs. This was in response to the noise he had made when he blew the back door open. A man in black jumped down the final few stairs until he was fully facing him, and Hunter saw he was holding an automatic rifle. The assailant opened fire and sprayed bullets from side to side, peppering the walls and sending Hunter and the team diving for cover left and right into bedrooms. Hunter crashed down onto the floor in front of a large double bed but immediately sprang to his feet, finding himself standing with Amy and Jodie. Simeon, Volkov and the two other Guild members must have gone the other way.

He heard Volkov screaming in the corridor and then the sound of an MP7 being fired in the enclosed space. The sound was deafeningly loud, reverberating into the bedroom and hammering Hunter's eardrums. He could smell gun smoke, and he heard more screams. He charged forward to the open door, pausing momentarily in the cover of the doorframe before spinning around and opening fire from the other side of the corridor, opposite Volkov, who was taking cover in a similar position in the other room. The two men now ripped dozens of rounds into the

Illuminati man and blasted him back into a bathroom at the far end of the corridor where he crashed through the door and slumped dead over the toilet.

Droz pushed past Volkov and ran into the corridor with his machine pistol aimed and ready to fire. He ran to the foot of the stairs, spun around and opened fire on someone else Hunter heard descending the staircase. There was a blood-curdling scream and a crash and then Droz stepped aside as the man he had killed came tumbling down the stairs and landed in a heap at the bottom.

* * *

Blanco was sitting in the Guild's van because it had a better stereo than the SUV Simeon had hired. Now, with the backpack containing the sword on the seat beside him, he watched the battle raging inside the house as dusk descended over the Alps. He had been considering the various merits of traditional versus avant-garde pizza toppings, but also wished he could be in there, fighting alongside his teammates. He would volunteer in a heartbeat, but it was just too risky leave the sword alone, and even worse would be walking it right into the middle of the enemy's quarters. On the other hand, he was starting to feel his age and had occasionally worried about letting his friends down in the heat of battle.

*Don't be stupid, you've got plenty of fight left in you yet, man.*

He was considering if there was any truth to his own self-reassurance when he caught movement in the van's side mirror. At first, he thought he'd imagined it, but then he chided himself for his doubt. If he'd learnt one thing over his life it was to listen to your instincts. Backing this thought up, he saw movement again. It was back in the trees at the edge of the drive where the van was parked, a gentle but odd swaying of a branch, knocking some water drops from the lower branches of a fir tree.

He reached for his gun out of habit, but he hadn't carried a sidearm on a holster on this mission. Praying that as devout as they were, the Guild placed their lives not only in God's hands but also in the saving grace of firearms, he opened the glove box and was relieved to see a Glock 17. He thumbed the magazine release. It slid out smoothly enough and he saw it was fresh and fully loaded. Useful. He racked the slide, chambering a round, and ducked his head down to get a better look through the mirror.

No movement.

Then he checked the other mirror, just in time to see a man in black charging towards the van with a compact machine pistol raised into the aim. Halfway to the van, the man opened fire, spraying the coachwork with rounds and shattering the window inches from Blanco's face.

Blanco leaned down on the seat and brushed the glass away as the man opened fire again. He was attacking him while the others were inside the main house. It was time to step up. The safety of St Michael's sword was now in his hands alone.

\* \* \*

Everyone else left the bedrooms and followed Droz up the stairs at lightning speed before reaching the first floor where the living area was located. Hunter heard a gun open fire from somewhere above him, and then he saw the horrifying sight of Droz being raked with rounds and crashing back into a hatstand at the top of the stairs. Lacroix screamed in French and made it to the top of the stairs in seconds, spinning around and opening fire on the man who had killed his colleague. Still, back in the stairwell,

Hunter heard this other man scream and hit the deck. He counted four Illuminati men down and remembered Droz had said there were at least around half a dozen, plus Goga. The whole team was now assembled at the top of the stairs in the living area. Hunter saw movement behind a frosted glass window, but before he could assess who it was, Volkov opened fire, punching holes in the frosted glass and killing whoever was behind it.

'Are you crazy?' Hunter yelled. 'That could be Toussaint!'

Before Volkov could answer, another Illuminati man appeared behind the shattered frosted glass and opened fire with a machine gun, smashing what was left of the window into a million shards and firing hot lead down through the corridor in their direction. Hunter dived through the nearest doorway, which sent him crashing into a dining room. Spared the heat of battle for a few seconds, he changed his magazine and took a breath. Things were getting out of control and he was reminded of some of the action he had seen in the army. The memories invaded his mind like an enemy platoon, but then Amy and Jodie joined him in the room and he was even relieved to see Volkov a step behind them.

'Where the hell is Simeon?' Hunter asked. 'This is insane.'

Volkov nodded, out of breath and red-faced. 'He said he was going to find Goga and kill him for what he did to the mentor.'

'How many of these Illuminati guys are left alive?' Amy asked, frantically poking her head through the door to peer down the hallway.

Hunter grabbed her and pulled her back into the safety of the dining room. 'I don't know how many are left, but let's not find out by sticking our heads out into the corridor!'

Amy knocked his hand off her. 'I'm not a raw recruit, Max! I'm a trained FBI agent. I didn't put myself at any risk at all.'

Outside in the corridor, Hunter heard more heavy machine gunfire and screams, then there was silence. Amy led the team out into the area at the top of the stairs, and they all saw Simeon standing above the smoking corpse of Goga.

'I told you I was an asset to the team,' Simeon said. 'This is the bastards who have been holding the mentor hostage. *Alors*... he is a dead bastard now.'

'Your leg's bleeding!' Amy said.

Simeon waved it away. 'It is just a flesh wound. Goga got lucky.'

Hunter scanned the floor they were on. 'Are there any more of these Illuminati men alive?'

Simeon shook his head firmly. 'No, not in here, at least. Now I must go and find the mentor!'

After clearing the first floor, Simeon moved up the stairs to the second floor and Hunter and the others followed him up. With all the Illuminati dead, the search for Toussaint was a little less lethal, but Hunter was still on edge. He realised how hard he was gripping the weapon in his hand and that he was almost shaking from the adrenaline that had been pumped into his body after such a high-intensity gun battle. It took him back momentarily to similar moments in Afghanistan and Iraq, two places he chose deliberately not to remember as much as possible.

At the top of the stairs, Simeon called out in French for his mentor. They all heard an old man's voice calling out. Clearly, the mentor had not been gagged.

\* \* \*

Blanco knew he had to get out of the van. Only one of those rounds had to puncture the petrol tank and both he and the sword were on a one-way flight to heaven. That might suit the sword, and even the Archangel Michael, but Sal Blanco planned to stick around on Earth for a good while longer than the next few seconds.

The problem was, the guy outside the van had other ideas.

Another burst of fire raked up the rear of the van. Blanco leaned down closer on the seat and heard the bullets punching through the steel and chewing into the chassis. That wasn't right. The first gunman was located somewhere off to the van's front-right. Whoever was making this new assault was behind the van. That meant at least one other gunman, maybe more.

Blanco's assessment was confirmed when he heard the men shouting at each other in French, then more gunfire, still coming from the rear and off to the right. He twisted in the seat and pulled the left door handle, then he slammed his boot against the door and kicked it wide open. He slid out of the van, a shower of smashed window glass coming out with him, and saw what must have been a third gunman in the trees ahead of him. The man was armed with the same compact machine pistol as the guy he'd seen in the mirror. Blanco raised the Glock and fired once, dropping the lone figure to the woodland floor.

Blanco then fell to the ground, scanning under the van for any sign of the other two men. He saw one pair of boots off to his right – the man who had shot up the rear of the van – and now he was heading his way. He heard more French pass between them but still couldn't see the other assailant. Behind him up at the house, he heard heavy submachine gunfire and a bloodcurdling scream. He prayed it was no one he knew.

Blanco had no interest in playing fair. Three against one was not fair, so he now fired at the man's legs, blowing holes in his shins and sending him down to the icy ground where he now curled up into a ball and screamed in agony. Blanco jumped to his feet and made his way to the end of the van until he was just able to see the man, firing the Glock once and ending his misery.

That left one more.

He made himself known by firing on Blanco from the front end of the van. Blanco rounded the corner of the van and, using the rear for cover, worked out the final assailant must be in the trees on the other side of the drive. The two men exchanged fire until Blanco, at least, was out of rounds. He cursed, and was about to snatch up the weapon of the dead man behind him, when the other man ran screaming from the trees with a blade on his hand. That answered the question Blanco had about whether or not the other guy was out of bullets.

The man was on him in seconds. He was much younger but slighter, and the old Brooklynite gave himself good odds of coming out on top. But his enemy was no pushover and slashed the blade at him in rage, only just missing his throat by inches.

Blanco pulled his head back and sideswiped the next attack, reaching out with his hand and grabbing the offending wrist before pulling down hard so the man was forced into a kind of bow. Blanco played the next obvious move, bringing his leg up and driving his knee up into his face, breaking his nose and knocking him out. He crashed down onto the ground and the knife tumbled harmlessly out of his hand.

After removing all the weapons from the three assailants, and pausing for just long enough to be confident there was no further threat, Blanco brushed his hands clean and looked at the unconscious man, shaking his head. 'Maybe I can go back to thinking about pizzas now, if that's okay with you guys.'

Then he climbed back up into the battered, wrecked van and relaxed in his seat, his mind turning once more to the horrors of pineapple on pizza.

*  *  *

Hunter followed Simeon down a dark wooden corridor, the floorboards covered with what looked like a very expensive antique runner, until they reached the front room, which appeared to be some kind of study. A large window looked out over the beautiful French snowcapped mountains beyond, and hastily lashed to a chair in the corner with duct tape was an elderly man. Hunter guessed Goga had bundled the old man up to the top floor as soon as he had heard him blowing in the back door.

Simeon and Toussaint exchanged rapid French sentences as he cut through the tape and liberated his mentor. Then they hugged and shared a hearty mutual pat on the back. Hunter wondered if he didn't catch a tear in the eye of both men and then Simeon approached Hunter with the old man.

'Hunter, I want to thank you and the HARPA team for rescuing Professor Toussaint, the mentor of the Guild of St Michael.'

'It was nothing,' Hunter lied. 'But now you can repay us by helping us get our friends back.'

Toussaint smiled. 'Not only will I help you get your friends back from this Illuminati scum, but I think I can offer you much more. I think I can tell you a little bit about who they are and what they want with this sword.'

'I think we have a pretty good handle on that,' Hunter said.

'I'm not so sure that you do, young man,' Toussaint said. 'I think that you should listen more and talk less.'

Amy smiled. 'I've been telling him that for years.'

## 18

The team made their way back down the stairs until they stepped outside through the smashed back door. Things were a little saner now, so they went slowly back down the drive until they reached Droz's van, where Blanco was waiting nervously.

Simeon shook his head. 'I can't believe those bastards murdered Jules and Henri!'

Toussaint stopped suddenly, looking at Simeon in absolute horror. 'Jules and Henri came here to rescue me?'

Simeon's face seemed to fall into shadow, and he nodded dumbly. 'They were very brave, Mentor, but they weren't careful enough. The Illuminati cut them both down dead.'

'This is terrible news,' Toussaint said. 'We are a tiny organisation and now we are made even smaller. Eventually, there will be none of us left. I must telephone their families immediately.'

'Not now, Mentor,' Simeon said. 'First we must get away from this place.'

The old man looked confused, staring at the house with a lack of comprehension, then bumbling about where he stood, wringing his cold, grey hands. *'Oui... tu as raison, mon fils.'*

When they got to the vans, they were shocked to find the Guild's vehicle was blasted to pieces. Blanco was standing beside their own SUV, parked up a few metres in front of it.

'All went well for you guys?' Blanco asked innocently.

Hunter looked down at the unconscious man. 'What the hell happened out here, Sal?'

'These guys interrupted an important new pizza topping I'd almost perfected, that's what.'

Toussaint was horrified. '*Mon Dieu!*'

'We need to get going,' Amy said, bringing everyone to order. 'We're not safe here.' Except for Blanco, who now opted to keep a single handgun on him until they reached the Altiport, the team threw the weapons in the back of Droz's wrecked van, grabbed the pack containing the sword and then made their way a little further down to the SUV Simeon had hired at the Altiport. They had anticipated the need for an eight-seater, knowing Droz and Lacroix had their own van, not that either man would be needing it now, Hunter considered grimly.

'Before we leave,' Toussaint said quietly, 'please may I see the sword? It is my life's work, after all, and if something were to happen to it... or me, before I had a chance...'

'Yes, but fast,' Amy said.

Hunter took some pleasure in watching Toussaint's face as he took in the full splendour of the ancient relic, and some small part of him hoped he would speak a little more about it, shed more light on their situation, but after wiping a tear from his eye, the old man returned the sword to Blanco and they all went over to the SUV. 'The symbols are interesting.'

'You know what they say?' Amy asked.

He nodded. 'They merely repeat the prophecy.'

Simeon's eyes darted to him, but Hunter saw he was too nervous to go further.

'Can we talk about the prophecy?' Amy asked.

The old man made a strange face. 'Perhaps, but this is neither the time nor place.'

Amy agreed. 'Let's get out of here.'

Jodie climbed into the driver's seat and fired up the engine. The others piled in, closed the doors, and buckled up while Jodie switched the heater fans on full and the SUV began to warm up.

There was a strange atmosphere inside the SUV, one Hunter was more than a little familiar with. On the one hand, they were jubilant that they had taken out a large number of Illuminati operatives and had managed to rescue Professor Toussaint. On the other hand, two good men had lost their lives in the battle. It was a feeling that was depressingly familiar to Hunter after so many missions with HARPA.

Jodie carefully turned the SUV out of the area they had parked in and rolled it down to the main road. Then she gradually increased speed as they headed back to the Altiport. Hunter had started talking about the urgency to get back to the mission to rescue Quinn, but Jodie interrupted him after seeing something suspicious in her rearview mirror.

'Guys, I don't know how to tell you this… but I think we're being tailed.'

'What?' Amy asked, turning around in her seat and squinting through the dirty rear window. 'I thought we took them all out back at the chalet?'

'I took out three,' Blanco said. 'I thought that was all of them.'

Hunter was upfront with Jodie. He dipped his head and looked in his own rearview mirror. 'Are you talking about that white Mercedes, Jodie?'

Jodie nodded. 'I sure am, Hunter. As soon as we pulled out of the chalet grounds, I saw it parked up. The second we moved away from the chalet it started driving behind us and it's been tailing us ever since. I think Goga must have managed to get the word out about our attack.'

'Oh, joy,' Blanco said. 'If losing two men wasn't bad enough, they're still on our tails.'

The next thing they knew, the passenger in the Mercedes had rolled his window down and opened fire on them with a handgun. The bullets punched holes through the rear window of the SUV and caused Jodie to swerve all over the road to stop those sitting in the back from being hit. Barely able to control the vehicle as it swerved and skidded on black ice, she now struggled to hold it steady as she ploughed through a deep puddle at the side of the road, only just managing to stay on the road.

'Is there another way to the Altiport?' Amy asked.

Toussaint, visibly shaken by the attack, nodded quickly. 'Yes, if we take the next right we can get there by driving behind the Hôtel Mercure. It avoids the main part of the resort.'

'You heard him, Jodie!' she said.

Jodie spun the steering wheel and turned the SUV so hard it momentarily tipped up onto two wheels. It crashed down with a suspension-crunching smack as Jodie straightened the wheel and stamped on the gas, rocketing the vehicle along a narrow road lined with fir trees. In the back, Amy lowered her window and twisted in her seat.

'I can't see them.'

Jodie checked the mirror. 'No, but they don't need three guesses to know where we're going. I think we can expect a welcoming committee at the Altiport if we don't get there very fast indeed.'

'This is madness!' Toussaint said. 'This must stop at once before someone gets killed. Never in my life have I known such violence.'

'I envy you, Professor,' Amy said. 'But you should prepare for much worse.'

'And lots of people have already been killed – including two of your own Guild members,' Blanco said. 'What we're trying to do is stop anyone else getting killed. Sadly, the guys who held you hostage at the chalet have different ideas. Taking innocent lives means nothing to them. Actually, we think they enjoy it.'

Toussaint withdrew into himself, quietly pondering Blanco's words. When he spoke, he shocked everyone with what he said.

'If you believe this, Mr Blanco, then you know your enemy only too well. These people have always enjoyed taking innocent, good life. They are the embodiment of pure evil and that is why it is so important we do not stoop as low as them, that we do not become them in our efforts to fight them.'

'That's a great sentiment,' Jodie said, checking her mirror. 'But sometimes you don't get a choice. Take my word for it as an ex-thief who lived in the real world, not locked away in some academic cloister like you do. No offence.'

'None taken, I'm sure,' said Toussaint, raising his palms. 'I just meant we must not lose our own souls in the fight against these evil men and women.'

'Sure, and I agree,' Amy continued, 'up to a point, but sometimes you have no choice. It's kill or be killed, or even worse, kill or let the other guy kill innocent people. I can't let that happen, not ever. I couldn't sleep at night. That's why I joined the FBI and that's why I joined this team. What we do matters and what we do is good, even if sometimes we have to hurt or take a life. That right there is the business end of the jungle, Professor.'

Volkov reached out and put a hand on her shoulder. 'You nearly brought tears to my eyes.'

'Shut your pie hole, Volkov,' Jodie said.

Before Volkov could reply, something Hunter saw he desperately wanted to do, the man in the Mercedes fired again, this time drilling holes in the back of the SUV's steel tailgate.

Blanco now pulled the handgun he had taken from the back of Droz's van, rolled his window down, unbuckled his seatbelt and leaned almost comically far out of the window before firing on the Mercedes. He unloaded the entire magazine, and Hunter watched through the mirror as the rounds ripped into the grille, blew up the radiator, split open the driver's side tyre, and punched a line of holes in the windscreen, killing both men. The Mercedes swerved and skidded off the road, smashing through a crash barrier, and then roared over the side of the mountain. It tumbled and smashed and rolled its way hundreds of feet below where it finally came to a smoking steaming heap at the bottom of the valley.

'Good shooting, Sal,' Hunter said, impressed.

'I think we have to get out of this place real damn fast,' Amy said. 'Because if the cops catch up with us we're gonna be spending a hell of a lot of time in France.'

'There's more of them!' Jodie cried out. 'There's a BMW approaching fast!'

'Then we have to get out of here even faster than I previously thought!' Amy said.

Toussaint made the sign of the cross. 'God protect us!'

As if on cue, Jodie now blew through the Altiport's entrance and brought the car to a swerving, juddering halt just yards away from the aircraft they had flown in on.

'Everyone, to the aeroplane!' Simeon called out.

'Maybe we should go through the airport first,' Amy said, conflicted. 'Do things right.'

'Are you insane?' Hunter said. 'Let's just get the hell out of here and if you're that bothered about it, maybe you can email the French authorities later and tell them what you did.'

'Sorry...' Amy said. 'It's a reflex.'

Hunter now followed the rest of the team as they abandoned the SUV with its doors open and its engine still running, and sprinted across the small car park before vaulting over a low brick wall and running to Simeon's aircraft.

'The BMW is heading this way!' Jodie called out. 'Everyone inside, now!'

# 19

Being the slimmest and smallest, Jodie was forced to squeeze down in between Amy and Toussaint in the middle row of seats in the Diamond DA62. The powerful turboprop could be configured for seven people, but this one was arranged only for six. It didn't take long for everyone to agree that sacrificing a little comfort was probably not such a bad thing when escaping from men firing automatic weapons at them. The BMW now pulled up beside their SUV and two men leapt out, each one drawing a handgun and firing on them as Simeon raced the aircraft down the runway.

'Is not optimal,' Volkov said. 'Take off now.'

'It doesn't work like that!' Simeon said. 'We have to wait until we have enough lift!'

At the end of the short, sloped runway, and with bullets chewing into the tarmac all around him, Simeon pulled back on the yoke and flew the aircraft up into the air over the valley with a ferocious roar of the turboprop engine. In seconds, the small resort far behind them looked more like a collection of toy houses and chalets, and the BMW and its occupants were no more than a memory. Turbulence buffeted the small plane as the two 2.0-litre turbocharged diesel engines powered them away from the danger back at Courchevel and into the cold sky. They went higher, punching through the thin, wispy cloud ceiling, and finally emerged into an aerial world of violet dusk skies and the powder-pink snow-caps of the surrounding Alps.

'Quite a view, eh?' Simeon said through the comms.

'I'm just praying no one put a nine-mil round through the gas tank,' said Jodie.

Amy shifted in her seat and pushed her over a bit. 'Always the romantic. Have you ever considered writing poetry?'

'Have you ever considered not crushing me into our guest?'

Toussaint smiled as he pulled out his notes. 'It's quite all right. I don't mind at all.'

'That's what I'm worried about,' Jodie muttered.

The plane's seating was configured with two seats at the front, two in the middle and two at the rear, with all six facing forward like in a family car. Simeon and Hunter were sitting up front, then Amy, Jodie and Toussaint in the middle, and Blanco and Volkov in the rear. After a short while, the adrenaline dissipated and everyone began to settle into the flight. It was mostly a smooth one, but occasionally the small plane rocked gently with turbulence. Outside, the sun dropped below the horizon. The pink snow-caps were slowly turning purple with the gathering dusk. High above, a wild grove of stars was scattered like stolen diamonds in the deep violet vault of night sky stretching all around them, seven wandering souls racing up to ten thousand feet above eastern France.

Simeon set the autopilot controls for the next waypoint and swept his eyes over the glass cockpit instrument panel one more time before finally sinking back into his seat and relaxing a little. Flying an aircraft demanded constant vigilance, but some parts of the flight were more stressful than others. Having safely escaped the Illuminati men back in Courchevel, navigated the turboprop out of the mountains and set a course for Berlin, he was able to take things a little easier. He turned to smile at Amy behind him.

'Could you pass the first-aid kit? I need to dress the flesh wound in my leg.'

'Sure thing,' Amy said, handing it over to him.

As Simeon started to dress the wound on his thigh, Amy turned to Toussaint. 'If you don't mind, Professor Toussaint – you were going to tell us something more about the Illuminati?'

Toussaint nodded, his face growing sombre. 'Yes, this is true. But the first thing to understand is there are so many different groups who describe themselves with this strange word, Illuminati. In the case of Oriax, we need to understand some very ancient things. The Illuminati have these days become more like a cult, if you will. They can mean anything to anyone. I think Oriax is a religious extremist who believes he is illuminated by God and charged with the salvation of mankind, by fire, if necessary. He may also worship Lucifer. I am not certain.'

'He's a Satanist then?' Hunter asked. 'I never saw that coming.'

Toussaint removed his glasses and polished the lenses while he considered Hunter's words. 'Oriax is not necessarily a Satanist. You need to remember that there is a distinction between Lucifer and Satan. A fine line, but a difference.'

Hunter looked confused. 'You're going to have to explain that one a little more.'

'In the Old Testament,' Toussaint continued, 'Lucifer was an angel, serving God in Heaven as one of his spirit sons. He was expelled from Heaven with a host of other fallen angels following a battle with God.'

'A battle over what?' Jodie asked.

'Depends on who you ask,' Toussaint said. 'Some scholars say it was Lucifer's refusal to bow down to mankind following the creation of man. This is the view most often interpreted in the Eastern Orthodox versions of the *Life of Adam and Eve*, a collection of writings known as the Jewish Apocrypha, in which Lucifer was banished to Sheol. A similar view is also loosely held in the Islamic tradition, when Iblis, the Islamic leader of the devils, also refuses to bow down to Adam.'

'The Islamic tradition is so similar?' Hunter asked. 'I had no idea.'

'Very similar,' Toussaint said. 'In the Quran, Iblis was expelled from Heaven in the same way as Lucifer, and for pretty much the same reasons, if you follow that scholarly interpretation, but there are others. Origen of Alexandria, an early Christian scholar working in the third century, offers the theory that Lucifer was expelled from Heaven after turning his back on God and orchestrating a rebellion. Or you can go with the idea John Milton came up with in "Paradise Lost" instead. He says the expulsion happened because Lucifer refused to be subject to the Messiah, God's son. One thing just about everyone agrees on is that he was an angel, expelled from Heaven. The name Lucifer has a specific meaning. It means the morning star, which is of course the planet Venus. This is probably a reference to his senior rank within the Lord's angelic host. And that is no small achievement. The Book of Revelation tells us the angelic host numbers ten thousand times ten thousand, which even my infamously poor mathematical abilities can work out is one hundred million. One hundred million angels and Lucifer was at the very top! By all accounts, he was handsome and possessed great wisdom. Bestowed with much influence and power, he was also described in the Book of Ezekiel as the Guardian Cherub. But these names were only used to call him when he was in Heaven. After the expulsion, he assumed another moniker altogether.'

'Satan,' Amy said.

Toussaint's eyes lit up. 'The Accuser.'

'Why the Accuser?' Jodie asked.

Hunter spoke up. 'Because Satan accused Job of believing in God only because he led such a blessed life.'

'Yes, but also no,' Toussaint said.

Hunter looked confused 'Eh?'

'This is one reason why Satan is called the accuser, but there is much more to it than that.'

'You're not getting any closer to winning that cigar, Hunter,' Jodie said with a smirk.

'I don't even smoke,' Hunter said with a shrug.

Toussaint ignored the banter and continued his explanation. 'Satan is called the Accuser because every time a man or woman sins, he accuses us of the sin before God and the Lord hears every word that Satan speaks. He hears every accusation of every sin. It is written in Revelation, chapter 12, verse 10: "And I heard a loud voice saying in heaven, Now is come salvation, and strength, and the kingdom of our God, and the power of his Christ: for the accuser of our brethren is cast down, which accused them before our God day and night." So you see, Satan's works are ceaselessly evil. Endlessly evil.'

The hum of the plane's engines filled the silence.

'And you think Oriax worships Lucifer?' Amy asked.

'It's possible he believes Lucifer is the true God.'

'Who would worship something so evil?' Jodie muttered, looking out of the plane's window at the moonlit mountain peaks in the distance. 'Those old engravings of the Devil with his wings and horns don't exactly make him look like the true God.'

Toussaint twisted his head to look at her. 'It wasn't until Dante, writing in the fourteenth century, that we see the Devil really taking shape as a winged beast. Dante was probably borrowing these descriptions from early Babylonian legends, many of which contain dragons and so on. In Inferno, he describes these wings not as those of a bird, but as those of a bat. He's channelling underworld imagery here. He wants us to loathe Satan as much as possible. And, of course, this works.'

'I always think of something like a goat,' Hunter said. 'Or is that just me?'

'It's not just you. The horns and goat imagery have a long pedigree, stretching back further than Alighieri's bat-winged beast. If you are ever in Ravenna, in north-eastern Italy, and you wander down a charming little road called the Via di Roma, you will find yourself looking at a beautiful basilica church. They call it the Basilica of Sant'Apollinare Nuovo. Theodoric the Great, the Ostrogoth King, had it built in the sixth century. If you go in summer, you step inside and get out of the heat. In the winter, you are grateful to be inside out of the wind. God welcomes you into his house, whatever the time of year, and inside, you will see an amazing display of ancient mosaics. One of them depicts Lucifer, as he was before the expulsion. Here, he is merely the original rebel angel, or the fallen angel, not the demonic beast he was gradually turned into over so many centuries by man's terrified imagination. If Oriax worships Lucifer, then it is the angel depicted in this mural that he worships, not the winged creature of Dante.'

'Do you really believe Oriax worships Lucifer?' Blanco asked quietly.

Toussaint shrugged. 'Perhaps. Oriax is a very warped man. He believes in God, but does he believe Lucifer is God? We cannot know his mind. This is why we cannot let him take the sword of the Archangel Michael. We can imagine what he plans to do with it. I think he wants to try to use it to bring Lucifer into our world.'

Hunter wondered if he was imagining the conversation. 'I

think I need to sleep. If this conversation gets any more insane, people can fill me in on what I miss when we get to Berlin.'

And with that, Hunter settled down into his seat with his arms crossed over his chest and closed his eyes. The engine hummed, and his friends chatted quietly in the low-lit cabin. The stars sparkled like brilliant white points, impossibly out of reach above the snowy peaks. All the talk of swords and gods and devils and power-hungry lunatics gradually drifted from his mind, and then he was asleep.

## 20

Despite the time being a little after 11.00 p.m., Berlin Brandenburg Airport was quieter than Hunter had presumed, and they quickly made their way to the short-stay car park. Professor Toussaint had made a call from the plane as it approached Berlin and promised them he could arrange transportation. He proved to be as good as his word, and a black Nissan Pathfinder was waiting for them there, delivered, as promised, by a member of the Guild of St Michael's German Chapter. They walked across the nighttime car park, their breath billowing out in front of them, all of them wishing they had warmer clothes.

'And it's all paid for, too?' Jodie said, climbing in behind the wheel. 'Winner, winner, chicken dinner.' She fired up the engine and got the heaters running, momentarily steaming up the windscreen. 'And who knew Berlin got so cold?'

'Not as cold as the reception we will get at Spionage,' Toussaint said, fumbling around next to Amy in the back as he tried to organise his seatbelt. 'Nachtnebel is not to be played with. If you think of Europe's various criminal networks as a giant web, he is the fat, black spider in the middle of it all, just waiting for someone to touch one of his many threads.'

'We are not going to gently touch a thread,' Hunter said. 'We're going to punch a hole right through the middle of his web.'

Toussaint slotted the seatbelt latch plate into the buckle with a satisfying clunk and regarded Hunter with a grave look on his elderly face. 'You say that as if you can just walk in there and play with this man. This is not likely, and even if you manage it, he will come after you. He will not let you be. Even the Guild stays away from Nachtnebel.'

'Although our paths rarely cross, Mentor,' Simeon said.

'No, thanks be to God.' Toussaint again made the sign of the cross.

Jodie followed the GPS data that they had programmed into the Pathfinder's computer and made the journey from Brandenburg Airport to the nightclub. It was situated just across the former border of East-West Berlin and now they cruised past the old Checkpoint Charlie, today set up as a tourist magnet. Hunter marvelled at the small gatehouse and a pile of sandbags, a mere shadow of the former Soviet Empire at the heart of Berlin, just a stone's throw away from McDonald's and endless coffee shops. Hunter stared out of his window and saw a large white painted sign on the right-hand side of the street telling him he was leaving the American Sector, and then Jodie turned right and drove for another minute or two to turn into a side street and pulled the car up on the pavement.

'I don't think you can park here,' Simeon said.

'We can park wherever we want,' Jodie said. 'No one around here cares if we get a parking ticket, and if they clamp the car or tow it away we'll just get another one. Does that allay your concerns?'

Volkov laughed, but Toussaint and Simeon seemed to take the

matter of obeying local traffic regulations far more seriously, by the look on their faces.

'Sal, you're on sword duty again,' Amy said.

Blanco nodded. 'Suits me.'

Hunter and the rest of the team climbed out of the car and the minute they were standing in the dark lamplight, they could immediately hear the deep thud of drums and the low growl of a bassline coming from inside the building in front of them.

'I bet it's been a while since you were in a place like this?' Jodie asked Hunter.

'Yes, thank God,' Hunter said.

'The last time you were in a place like this, this city was still divided into East and West Berlin, I expect.'

Hunter looked at Jodie with a withering expression on his face. 'It's not quite that bad.'

'But almost, I'll bet.'

Jodie was first to walk up to the bouncers and stepped inside the nightclub door out of sight. There was no queue because they had arrived late and the initial surge of people wanting to get inside the club had already passed. Entering, they immediately found themselves inside a dark red plush-carpeted lobby. The bass boomed louder in here as Amy walked up to the office and paid for everyone to get in.

'That's very kind of you,' Volkov said, placing his hand on the counter for the woman to stamp. When Hunter received his stamp, he looked down and saw it was a large S, for Spionage.

'I'm surprised they don't verify you bought the tickets by an eye scan stored on a server in Iceland. The stamp is reassuringly old-fashioned.'

He turned and followed Amy through two double doors. They were painted in matte black and were good sound insulators because the moment he pushed through them, the drums and bass became ten times louder. He was standing at the top of the carpeted stairs. Like in the lobby, the walls and the carpet were all blood red. Amy was already halfway down, and Jodie was behind her. The rest of the team were behind Hunter and now he made his way down to the bottom of the stairs where there was another small lobby. Off to the right he saw some kind of quiet room, ladies' and gents' toilets and another room marked as private, which he presumed led off to the management offices. To his left, where Amy and Jodie were already standing, was another set of dark black double doors, and he looked through two small windows at the top of them to see a hellscape of flashing red and white lights.

'I think I'd rather get shot on the Eiffel Tower than go in there,' he said, and meant it.

'Well, you're going in there, old man!' Jodie said, grabbing him by his elbow.

Hunter resisted. 'How about you go in there and I'll go down and look in what is obviously Nachtnebel's private office suite over there to the right?'

'Because we're going to go in here and pretend that we're regular punters,' Amy said.

Simeon gave Toussaint a doubtful look as the old Guild of St Michael mentor laughed at the prospect of himself being a 'regular' in a place like this. 'I'm in my sixties, Miss Fox!' he said in his strong French accent. 'I don't think there'll be too many like me behind those doors.'

'You're dressed all in black,' Amy said, trying to make him feel better. 'I think you'll fit in just great. You can play the part of an eccentric billionaire, and if that doesn't work, you'll still blend in better than Max here.'

floor, captivated by the hundreds of beautiful young women dancing the night away. 'This reminds me of Russian nightclub. Maybe you go after Nachtnebel and I stay here and keep all the beautiful women happy.'

Jodie laughed, and not in a good way. 'Good grief.'

Volkov gave her a dirty look and then Amy spoke up, diverting the chat back to business.

'Listen, we know that Nachtnebel is the Illuminati man who was running Floquet, and therefore the man who organised the bombing at the warehouse that nearly killed us. We also know that he is the last stepping stone between us and Oriax. He's either in his nightclub tonight, which we know he usually spends a lot of time in because he likes to be in the club when it's running, or there's someone in here who knows where he is. I suggest we just settle down for a second, study the layout of this place and then try to find him. Max might be right; he's probably in the private office suite.'

'I usually am right,' Hunter said with an exaggerated wobble of his head.

'You're not right this time,' Jodie said with pleasure. 'Look down there.'

Hunter looked down through the glass booth over the rail and onto the heaving dance floor. He was amazed to see Werner Nachtnebel, a tall, thin man with a shock of white hair, wearing a dark black suit and white shirt, strolling through the middle of the dance floor without a care in the world. Flanked by four men who were clearly close protection, Nachtnebel moved like a god, the men and women on the dance floor parting for him as if he were Moses and they were the Red Sea. The image was further enhanced in Hunter's mind by the fact that most of the lights flashing on them were red.

Amy watched Nachtnebel carefully. 'Well, look at that. If the

mountain won't go to Mohammed, then Mohammed must come
to the mountain.'

'What next?' Jodie asked.

'We go down there and have a chat with him,' Simeon said.
'Nothing could be easier.'

Somehow, Hunter doubted that.

## 22

Hunter put his empty lager bottle down on the table, reluctantly stood up and opened the booth door. Everyone else followed him out and then they filed back down along the walkway and made their way slowly down the staircase on the side of the dance floor. Hunter never took his eye off Nachtnebel the entire time he was walking and when he reached the dance floor level, he saw the German nightclub boss and Illuminati kingpin, plus his coterie of goons, making his way off to the far left of the stage where there was another door, this time guarded by two more heavy-duty bouncers.

'What do you think is through there?' Amy asked, raising her voice to be heard over the music.

Hunter went to reply but then was almost knocked off his feet by a dancer behind him. He straightened himself up and leaned into Amy. 'Could be more offices, or maybe some kind of VIP area.'

'It doesn't look like we can just walk through there though,' Amy said.

Hunter studied the two doormen. 'I think between HARPA,

Volkov and Simeon we can get through those two clowns on the door. Follow me.'

With the music pounding all around them, Hunter led the team once again on another journey, this time to the far end of the dance floor, raising his hands to his ears and putting his fingers in his ears as they walked past the Stonehenge of Bass, and then turned the corner rounding the edge of the stage and approaching the two men guarding the door. Hunter looked at the sign now and saw silver letters on the door saying: PRIVAT. This didn't give him a clue as to whether it was a private office suite or a VIP area, but its location suggested the latter.

As he neared the door, one of the two men stepped forward and raised his hand. He leaned forward and spoke to Hunter in German, a language Hunter knew poorly. He caught almost nothing at all apart from 'kein Eintrag', which he knew from a wonderful young woman from Düsseldorf whom he once dated meant 'no entrance'. It was a private joke.

Hunter was searching through the deep records of his mind back to when Elsa from Düsseldorf had taught him a thing or two, including some German, to explain to the man that he was indeed a Very Important Person and probably should be allowed to go through the doors. The small progress he was making was broken when Volkov pushed past him and slammed the heel of his right hand up into the man's chin, knocking his head back, and then punched him in the stomach with his left hand, bringing him back down again. Without waiting a heartbeat, or even for the other man to react, Volkov immediately swung his right hand around, catching the other man in the side of the head with the back of his hand. Then he rotated around, twisting at his waist and bringing his left leg up, connecting with the second man's stomach and winding him badly. Then he punched the second man in the head with his right hand before spinning around and kicking the first man in the head with his right foot. The entire thing took less than ten seconds and now both the bouncers were unconscious on the floor.

He glowered at Hunter. 'Russians act, not talk.'

Hunter couldn't argue with that, especially after what he had just seen. He followed Volkov through the double doors into the space behind. Simeon and Toussaint dragged the two unconscious bouncers through the doors and lay them side by side on the other side, so as not to alert anyone on the dance floor to what had just happened, although most seemed to be out of their minds anyway.

Hunter looked around his new surroundings and saw they were standing in another carpeted lobby area, only this time everything was decorated with gold and black. The carpet was rich and thick, and black and white photographs of Cold War Berlin hung on the walls in gold frames. Even the door handles were golden.

'Three doors,' Simeon said.

'Which one did Nachtnebel use?' Amy asked.

Hunter shrugged. 'Search me. There's nothing even written on any of them. We could push one of those doors and catch Nachtnebel on the shitter.'

Amy gave him a look of barely concealed disgust, but Volkov laughed heartily and slapped him on the back.

'Is funny.'

Hunter thought so too, and now the team decided to go through the door on the far left first and see what they could find. Hunter was first, and he pushed through the door but found nothing more than a small office with a desk up against the far wall and a row of three filing cabinets beside it. It was dark and the room looked unused. Pushing back out of the door, he reported his findings to the rest of the team, and they decided to move on to the next door.

Hunter pushed this door open and was met with a highly different experience. It was only halfway open when a hand reached out of nowhere, grabbed a fistful of his shirt around his neck and pulled him violently into the room. The Englishman was aware of being forced to the floor at high speed. His face crashed into cold tiles then he felt somebody kicking him in the ribs. After that, chaos exploded. The door behind him, through which he had just been dragged, burst open and Volkov and the rest of the team stormed into view. Hunter was still gasping for breath, and he twisted his head to see boots running all over the place. He started to crawl up to his hands and knees and felt another boot kick him in the ribs from the other direction, sending him right back down again. There were gunshots. Screams. He heard the sound of people being punched and hit and struck all over the room. He had to join the fight.

Hunter checked around him and saw whoever had kicked him in the ribs had run off to join the fight. He now jumped up to his feet and stormed towards a man in a grey suit. As he approached the man, he took the room in for the first time. It was poky and dimly lit and there were several tables stacked with massive piles of cash – euro banknotes stacked up one or two feet high wherever he looked. The man he had approached now swung a punch at him. Hunter ducked, allowing the man's fist to sail over his head, and then he piled his right fist forward, driving it into the man's stomach. His fist met a wall of iron, and the man laughed. He grabbed another fistful of Hunter's jacket and pulled him up closer before swinging his fist and punching him in his stomach. Hunter felt like he'd been hit with a bat and doubled over again, crashing down onto the floor and trying to heave air into his lungs.

'You didn't learn the first time?' the man said, laughing again. 'This will be fun.'

Hunter was coughing wildly and seriously considering the possibility that he might be about to pass out when he looked up at the man. Blond hair, ice-blue eyes. He recognised him immediately as one of the men who had walked across the dance floor beside Nachtnebel. Hunter was considering the best way to take on someone who must have weighed at least twice as much as him and with considerably chunkier muscle tone when Volkov sprang into view, grappled with the man and threw him down to the floor in the kind of dump tackle that would get you barred from playing rugby for life. Hunter wasn't complaining, as Volkov's bravery gave him time to jump to his feet and scan the room and try and make sense of what was happening. Everywhere he looked was some kind of a fistfight; even Jodie was getting stuck in, fighting a man who was standing in front of an open safe, and Amy was fighting a woman in a corner office, visible only now and again when the two brawling women moved in front of an internal window partially blocked by a Venetian blind.

To the side of the office where Amy and the woman were fighting, Hunter saw Nachtnebel shoulder-barging his way through a fire door. He was holding two massive bags full of something in his hands. Whatever it was, it wasn't cash – it looked more like stones or rocks, and Hunter's first thought was precious stones. Simeon had also seen Nachtnebel, and he and Toussaint, who had been standing timidly with his back up against the wall and watching the fight unfold around him in horror, now took off after the German Illuminati chief. The fight in this room had come to an end, and HARPA and their allies had been victorious. Volkov landed the last punch, almost running his fist through the middle of the head of the man with ice-blue eyes and knocking him back onto a filing cabinet. He slumped down onto the ground with his eyes closed and his head limply hanging down over his chest.

'He will not fight again tonight,' Volkov said.

'Never mind that!' Amy said. 'Nachtnebel just went through that door! He's getting away!'

## 23

The fire door led to an alleyway at the back of the nightclub. Standing in a refreshing drizzle, Hunter scanned up and down and caught the strange vision of Werner Nachtnebel sprinting across slick cobblestones on his way to a black Mercedes limousine parked up at the end of the alley. With the nightclub still pulsing and pounding behind him, and the noise of the bass and drums spilling out into the street, he turned to Amy and the others who had now gathered around him and pointed at Nachtnebel.

'He's got a car down there!' he said, his breath condensing in the cold air as he spoke.

'We can't let him get away,' Amy said. 'He is the end of the trail as far as any hope of rescuing Quinn and the others is concerned.'

The team took off after Nachtnebel, but two outliers immediately presented themselves. Toussaint was last, struggling to reach anything more than a fast walk, and rapidly dropped behind the rest of them. The second was Volkov, who now took off like an Olympic one hundred metres champion, rapidly catching up with Nachtnebel and once again replaying his rugby tackle, leaping into the air and bringing the Illuminati chief crashing into the cobblestones with a sickening smack.

Hunter and Amy exchanged a glance of admiration for the brave Russian as they ran down the alley, and by the time they caught up with him, he had turned Nachtnebel onto his back and dragged him up so he was sitting up against the wall of the alley-way. Blood streamed from his smashed nose and split lips.

Hunter, trying hard to conceal how breathless he was in front of Amy, walked up to Nachtnebel and looked at him with disgust. 'How could you do it?'

'*Was?*' Nachtnebel said in German, looking at him with inno-cent eyes. 'It's just a simple money-laundering operation!'

'No,' Hunter said, gradually getting his breath back. 'I meant to decorate your nightclub like that! I've never seen such retro horrors in all my life.'

Amy rolled her eyes and pushed Hunter out of the way. 'What he means is, where the hell are you keeping our people?'

Nachtnebel began laughing, a horrible, gravelly cackle. This enraged Amy, who kicked one of the bags he'd been carrying, and to Hunter's surprise, sprayed hundreds of diamonds out across the cobblestones. They rapidly disappeared into the water-filled grooves between the cobblestones. Nachtnebel gasped in horror and crawled away, trying to scrape them out of the gaps. 'What have you done? There are millions of euros worth of diamonds here! Are you insane?'

Amy showed how she felt about the matter by kicking the second bag in the other direction, spraying the rest of the diamonds just as widely as she had the first.

'She really is insane,' Jodie said.

'Forget about the diamonds, Nachtnebel!' Amy said as he continued to grovel about scraping them up. 'I'll kill you right here if you don't tell me where we can find our friends.'

He turned and grinned at her. 'Only Oriax knows where your friends are.'

'Well, then you'd better tell us where Oriax is, hadn't you?' Hunter said, stepping back into the conversation. He stared down at Nachtnebel, studying his white hair that had once been blond, his dark ice-blue eyes, and his lean face with a day or two's worth of stubble on it. As a younger man he would have been quite striking, but evil had consumed it and now he looked hollowed out and soulless.

'Who says I know where he is?'

Jodie stepped forward and kicked Nachtnebel hard in the stomach, making him wheeze and cough and roll around in the wet street. 'In that case, get on your damn phone and find someone who does know where he is.'

Nachtnebel was still sucking up water from the street as he waved his arm blindly in the air to stop Jodie from kicking him again. 'You don't understand! Oriax is never in one place for long. He is always being chased by someone! He has upset every gang in Europe and North America. He has enraged every criminal mastermind and kingpin in the world. Every government has him on their most wanted list. He can never stop moving, because he can never trust anyone. If he stays in the same place for too long, someone will give his location away and then he knows he will be killed.'

'Sounds like one hell of a life,' Amy said. 'What are you trying to tell us? That he flies around the world, from home to home?'

'He has got homes all over the world, but that is not where you will find him.'

'Sounds like you know where he is, after all,' Jodie said. 'Spit it out.'

Nachtnebel went still, staring at himself in a cold puddle inches from his face. Something in that reflection, something in those eyes staring back at him, made him change his mind. 'I tell you this only because he has betrayed me, cutting me loose and threatening to destroy everything I built for myself here in Berlin. He is a bastard and this is my chance for revenge. You will find him on board the Voskhodyashchaya Zvezda.'

'That's easy for you to say,' Hunter said, drawing another look of disappointment from Amy.

'It's Russian,' Volkov said. 'It means "rising star".'

'That is right,' Nachtnebel said. 'The Rising Star is his personal luxury train.'

Jodie whistled. 'This dude has a train?'

'It is more than a train,' Nachtnebel said. 'It is an enormous, sumptuous headquarters on wheels, pulled by a powerful former Soviet locomotive. It drags him back and forth across Russia and it never stops moving. It has everything on board that a man could want. It has a living area, a cinema, kitchens, a dining room, sumptuous bathrooms, bedrooms, guest bedrooms, a billiards room, a smoking room, and a study. You name it and it's on board the Rising Star. I went there once but not when it was moving. It was while it was in the station in Yekaterinburg.'

'And how do we find this train?' Hunter asked.

'You cannot find it. It never stops moving. I already told you that.'

Hunter was beginning to understand Amy's frustration with this man and almost felt like kicking him in his ribs himself. Maybe he was telling the truth about the Rising Star, but then again maybe he wasn't. He'd already shown what kind of man he was by grovelling around in the gutters trying to scrape up the diamonds that were presumably part of his money-laundering racket. Hunter felt mildly disappointed – he'd imagined an Illuminati kingpin behaving in an entirely different fashion. What he was looking at right now was nothing more than a local city gangster, who made his money through intimidating people or bullying them via protection rackets. He probably indulged in some theft and drug dealing on the side. If this was the kind of man Oriax hired to run one of his local crime regions, then maybe he had overestimated the enemy. Now he looked across at Simeon, who had been in a brief French conversation with Toussaint. He could see from the look on the young Frenchman's face that he felt roughly the same way about Nachtnebel as he did. Simeon now stepped forward with his fists balled tightly at his sides.

'He's lying!' Simeon said. 'Why don't we just kill him now? We can find some other way to get your friends back.'

Amy rounded on him. 'That's easy for you to say, Simeon! We already found your mentor. Our friends and colleagues are still being held hostage! That's why we're not just going to kill him here. Oh, yeah – also, we're not murderers!'

Hunter admired Amy's forthright response to the hot-blooded Frenchman, but he couldn't help but share a little sympathy with the way he felt. Simeon backed down, deferring to Amy's leadership role in the HARPA team, and walked back over to stand beside Toussaint, both men, like the rest of the team, now slick with water thanks to the drizzle drifting gently out of the cold Berlin sky.

'It is not murder when you kill a man like this!' Simeon said with disgust. 'Is it, Mentor?'

Toussaint gave Simeon a sad look. 'I'm afraid it would be murder, my son. You must control your temper if you are ever to rise in the ranks of the Guild.'

Nachtnebel began laughing wildly. 'The Guild! How many more of these pathetic little groups are there trying to take on the Illuminati? None of you can ever succeed. We are too powerful!'

'You're a bunch of psychopaths,' Jodie said.

'Where is the train?' Amy asked one more time. 'I don't believe it never stops moving, because it needs to resupply with fuel and food and water. Where is it?'

'Very well,' Nachtnebel said reluctantly. 'It normally runs between Moscow and Yekaterinburg, but there has been a change and Oriax has decided to take the train south instead of east. I don't know why. I know he will be leaving Moscow within the next twelve hours and the train will be going south, but that is all I know.'

'What station is it at?' Amy asked.

'Kursky, of course.'

Amy frowned at him. 'Why of course?'

Volkov answered for Nachtnebel. 'Because Kursky is biggest station in Moscow. Is main train station there and many trains leave there for all over Russia and outside of Russia. Big trains.'

Hunter said, 'I didn't think you could get trains direct from Moscow down to the Middle East.'

'That is because you're thinking of commercial trains,' Nachtnebel said. 'But this is a private train. He pays for the use of the line out of his practically limitless funds and can go wherever there are railway tracks. Believe me, it is more than possible to get from Moscow to Cairo or a good deal further in each direction.'

Amy now surprised everybody by giving Nachtnebel a brutal scissor kick, knocking him out where he sat. The German gangster slumped down onto the wet pavement beside his beloved diamonds.

'That was a little unexpected,' Hunter said.

Amy glared at the unconscious man. 'Someone call the Berlin police and tell them there's a pile of garbage here that needs to be collected. Don't forget to tell them about all of these diamonds and what we found back inside that office. The rest of you, get ready. We're flying to Moscow first thing in the morning.'

## 24

A little after twenty-four hours after the rest of HARPA had left Cornwall and headed to London, Quinn Mosley woke from her latest drug-induced stupor and knew immediately that she was on board a train, despite the hood over her head. They were not in motion, but she could hear other locomotives trundling past whatever carriage she was in, sometimes by just a few feet. She could feel their vibrations as they clicked over the points. She also heard men and women shouting in Russian. The clincher for her was when she heard an announcement being made about the departure of a train to Paris, made first in Russian, which she didn't understand, but then in English, which clarified the situation for her beyond doubt.

She was sitting in what felt like a private compartment, the sort that used to be common on trains many decades ago but not so much these days. Her hands were cuffed behind her back. This was her life now. She had been this way for somewhere between thirty-six and forty-eight hours – she could not tell how long any more. But she was able to stand up and shuffle around the small space. She determined its size by scraping the toe of her shoe around the walls and bases of the seats. She was satisfied that there was no one else in the compartment. Since she had lived her life with a hood over her head, it was amazing how paranoid she had become on the subject of people being in the same room as her and silently observing her. For once, she felt she was really alone.

Her mind filled with concerns about what had happened to Jim and Susanna Gates and Professor Bonnaire. Were they still alive? Had they been separated for some reason, or had Oriax ordered Jophiel to execute them before bringing her to the train? There was no way to tell, and that was the worst thing about her situation – the constant never knowing.

She sat back down in what she supposed was the seat by the window, as far away from the door as she could get, and arranged herself so her arms were as comfortable as possible, wedged behind her back with her hands cuffed. A small part of her began to give up on ever being rescued. She knew it was stupid and pessimistic. If it really had been only thirty-six hours since she had been snatched from the forest, then that was not a very long time for the rest of HARPA to mount a rescue operation. They could still be putting pieces together, finding whatever clues they could back at the forest, chasing leads; there was online research to consider... all of Amy's friends back at the FBI, Jim Gates and his CIA contacts. She doubted Hunter's archaeologist friends could be much use back at his university in England or UNESCO, but then maybe she was wrong. If this entire thing had been about what they were seeking, if this entire thing was about the sword, then maybe Hunter was the key to her rescue. Her mind was a mess.

She heard the door open. It was a heavy satisfying clunk, of proper old-fashioned brass workmanship and heavy hardwood. She guessed that meant this train was old or had been refurbished in a vintage style. She guessed her captor liked the finer things in life. Whatever this place was, it was certainly better than the basement they had held her in back when they had visited the United States. She didn't even know what state that had been. The door clicked shut and she knew the person who had opened it had come into the compartment because she heard someone sitting down on the seat opposite her. Then she heard breathing.

'Are you going to introduce yourselves or what?' she asked.

'It's just me, Jophiel.'

'How's it hanging, Jay?'

A pause. 'I know you must be feeling very angry, very frightened, but I have done my best to keep you alive.'

Quinn wasn't sure what to say. Superficially, she was of course immediately grateful, but then her mind got working. Perhaps this was all part of some mind-control game. Maybe this Jophiel was playing on some twisted good-cop-bad-cop thing that would come back to bite her. She didn't want to play the grateful, pathetic damsel in distress. So she chose her words carefully.

'What about the others? Have you kept them alive as well?'

'Where do you think you are right now?'

Quinn did not like the way he had changed subject so easily. She worried it meant that her friends had been executed after all, that they weren't here on the train but lying dead in a ditch somewhere. She wasn't sure whether to press the matter or go off in the direction he wanted her to. She decided for now not to aggravate him and play along with him instead.

'I believe I'm in a train compartment.'

'This much is easy to deduce,' Jophiel said. 'Especially for a woman of your intelligence and capability. But where do you think that train might be?'

'Russia,' she said, then qualifying herself, 'Or somewhere in the Russian Federation.'

She heard his clothes rustling. 'You heard the speaker out on the platform.'

'So what if I did?'

'It wasn't to be helped,' he said with regret in his voice. 'There was no way to soundproof the compartment, and it hardly matters anyway.'

'Why does it hardly matter?'

'Never mind.'

'So, the man who ordered me to be kidnapped is Russian then?'

'Yes. He is Russian and the owner of this train. It's called the Rising Star. It never stops moving except when it's time to make repairs or resupply with food, water and fuel. Oriax has a large staff of chefs, waiters, and personal attendants, not to mention his small army of private security and close protection guards, and they work on the Rising Star in a rotation system. Oriax himself rarely leaves the train, except when he must personally attend an Illuminati mission that may require his personal supervision, and of course to pray. He likes to go to church to pray.'

'I thought you Illuminati guys were all Satanists?'

Jophiel huffed out a sad laugh. 'More drivel brought to you courtesy of the television set, or I suppose these days the internet screen. No, Quinn – we are not all Satanists. I am not a Satanist and Oriax is not a Satanist. In fact, he is very far from a devil-worshipping maniac. Oriax believes profoundly in God and that is his greatest source of strength. That is why he wants the sword, not to commit some sacrilegious outrage against God, but to use it in the fight against evil wherever he finds it.'

'And what does Oriax mean when he thinks of evil?'

'The vile, sinful debauchery we see all over our world. The disgusting degeneracy is to be found everywhere we look. Oriax wants to rid the world of this filth, to purge the pestilence and return our glorious world to a simpler time when the division between good and evil was understood by everyone and everybody obeyed the word of the Lord God.'

'Is Oriax some kind of crazy evangelical extremist? It sounds like it to me.'

'That is because you are lost in a sea of evil.'

'If you say so.'

'I do say, and so does the prophecy.'

Quinn felt her blood run cold. 'Prophecy?'

Jophiel fell silent. 'An ancient prophecy, a divine prophecy.'

'Care to let the cat out of the bag?'

Oddly, his voice sounded almost warm. 'Even if I knew it, I would not. It would not be my place. Only Oriax knows the prophecy.'

'But you must have some idea?'

'It concerns the sword,' he said dreamily, 'and a terrible power given to anyone who controls it. I believe whoever wields the sword will become as powerful as God. This is the secret that was kept for so many centuries by those inside the Guild and the League.'

'I don't understand any of this. What are you talking about?'

He seemed to snap back into reality. 'Now I have said too much, but perhaps...' Jophiel now surprised her by rising from his seat and tearing the hood off her head. With no warning, her eyes, which had been mapping the strange folds and contours of her hood, her tiny black world, were suddenly illuminated by the bright daylight, which painfully stung her eyes and caused her to blink and curse.

'You could have warned me, man!'

'I'm so sorry, Quinn,' Jophiel said. 'I really didn't mean to cause you any pain.'

Quinn thought he sounded genuinely sincere, as he had done

on the other occasions when he had spoken to her – all except the first time when he was cold and menacing. Exactly who was the real Jophiel, she wondered. She supposed there was no way to know, and her best policy, her best chance of survival, was to play the man, however he appeared to her at the time.

'I believe you when you said you knew nothing of this so-called prophecy, but I also asked if Oriax was an evangelical extremist. Is that true?'

'And I gave you no response,' Jophiel said. 'Terms such as this mean nothing to Oriax. He does not come from your American culture and does not identify with any of its finer intricacies. Oriax is a devout believer in God and worships through his own church. He was perhaps a little naïve. I feel he may have believed that no one would try to stop him from taking the sword, for he believed that no one could possibly object to a man like him wanting to do the good work of the Lord with it.'

Quinn felt like she was watching one of those religious TV channels back in the States. She was not entirely convinced by Jophiel's explanation of Oriax as a harmless individual intent on doing the Lord's work. The simple act of her brutal kidnapping, the way she'd been treated, drugged and hooded as well as the same treatment meted out to Jim and Susanna Gates and Professor Bonnaire, was a far better indication of what was in his heart than the empty words spoken by one of his many minions.

'You could just let me go, you know,' she said, twisting so he was able to see her cuffed hands. 'I don't need any help after you've done that. I don't care if we're in Russia. I've got skills, Jay. I could be anywhere on Earth just so long as I get access to the internet and then I can work wonders.'

'I know who you are and what you're capable of,' Jophiel said. 'That is why you were snatched, so we would have the most valuable member of the HARPA team in our possession.'

'Why didn't you just take everybody?'

'Because at that moment HARPA had not yet secured the sword. It was decided from on high that they would be allowed to complete their mission, but we would obtain a little insurance for ourselves along the way.'

'Great... now I'm an insurance policy.'

Jophiel smiled. 'I already told you that I'll do everything I can to ensure no harm comes to you.'

'Yeah. So you said, but forgive me if I don't believe what you tell me. You are holding me captive right now, with my hands cuffed behind my back, and just a second ago I had a hood over my head! Now you sit here trying to talk to me like we're friends.'

'I have my orders, Quinn.'

'Why are you in here now?'

'I'm in here to tell you that we are going to be taking the train south to Egypt.'

'What's in Egypt? I'm guessing your Oriax dude doesn't want to go down there just so we can take some selfies in front of the pyramids?'

'Oriax has ordered the Rising Star to go south so that we can be in Egypt within the next few hours.'

'A few hours? I thought this was a train, not a plane!'

'It is a train, but a very fast one. It has a top speed of two hundred kilometres per hour. I'm afraid I can tell you nothing more than that because it is highly confidential. All you need to know is we have our reasons. So long as the rest of your team do as they are told and take the sword to the location of the trade in Cairo, then you will be returned to them along with the other hostages.'

Jophiel got up and left the carriage. She heard him turn a key in a lock. She was alone again.

Quinn somehow doubted what Jophiel had said about being

returned alongside the other hostages, but for now, she had to hold on to it. There was still no way she could see how to make her escape. Her hands were cuffed, and even with the hood removed, she was still sitting on board Oriax's personal train somewhere in the Russian Federation, a train that was about to start moving south presumably at high speed down to Egypt. She wondered if it might stop along the way, giving her a chance to escape at a station, but what if it didn't? Jophiel said it rarely stopped. Her heart sank, and then she also sank, back down into the seat. Her only hope was the prospect of Hunter, Amy, Sal and Jodie somehow finding her and breaking her out of this hell. She didn't know what god Oriax worshipped. She wasn't too sure what god she worshipped, or even if she believed in God at all, but now she closed her eyes and started to pray to anyone who might listen.

## 21

Everyone followed Amy through the double doors into the heaving, noisy nightclub on the other side. Hunter was surprised at the enormous size of the venue, not having been inside a place like this since he went to an old rave back in the early nineties, in an aircraft hangar somewhere in Gloucestershire. The difference was that this was indoors and heated, but it was still a massive crowd of jumping, spinning bodies, most of whom were much younger, lither and fitter than he was.

Laser lights, mostly red and white, zipped and flashed and strobed above their heads, occasionally lighting what seemed like an infinitely high ceiling of black industrial tubes and pipes and wires. The source of the noise was coming from a stage at the far end of the room, where a man in his thirties with shoulder-length hair was bobbing up and down, holding one half of a set of heavy-duty earphones to his right ear while twiddling buttons on a mixing desk in front of him. His mixing desk was flanked on either side by two speaker cabs that roughly shared the same dimensions as the large sarsen stones Hunter was very familiar with at Stonehenge. There were other speakers positioned behind the stage and more mounted on the walls. There was absolutely no escaping the racket, which to Hunter sounded like a cross between a piece of agricultural equipment in dire need of repair and a faulty fire alarm.

*Really am getting on a bit*, he thought with genuine regret. *Where did it all go?*

He saw Jodie was much more in her element, effortlessly making her way through the middle of the dance floor, which seemed to have a population density of three people per square metre. Even more disconcerting to Hunter was the fact that he was old enough to be the father of just about everybody he looked at, which did not do his notoriously smooth and large ego much good. Hunter was not above showing interest to women considerably younger than himself – the most recent attempt was an archaeologist student of his back in the beautiful abbey on Mont Saint-Michel – but something about this place, the sheer density of youth, once again made him feel just too old to be in here. He didn't belong in these places any more. He was an impostor.

Amy seemed to be fitting in somewhere in between him and Jodie and was managing even to move in time to the music as she followed Jodie across the dance floor. Blanco had certainly got lucky when Amy had asked him to stay behind in the car and watch the rucksack with the sword in it, and Hunter wished now more than anything he had volunteered to stay with him. He wanted to suggest it now, advancing the argument that Blanco might not be up to protecting the sword on his own, but as a former US Army helicopter pilot, and HARPA veteran of four previous missions, the New Yorker was more than capable of looking after himself and the sword in a city like Berlin. In the very worst-case scenario, he would simply fire up the Pathfinder and get the hell away from whatever was bothering him, before joining up with the team later. Looking around the heaving biomass, Hunter wished he was in that Pathfinder, even if it meant getting shot at, rather than being in here.

He saw from the faces of Volkov and Simeon that they felt roughly the same as he did, but strangely Mentor Toussaint seemed to be enjoying himself and was already bobbing his head up and down to the incessant bass beat coming from the far end of the room. Hunter picked up his pace as he weaved in and out of the squirming bodies, still jumping up and down in the flashing red and white lights, and soon found himself standing beside Amy Fox at a very long and brightly lit bar. This was a place of black marble and red underlighting, and the staff were all dressed in black. There were classy, vintage Cold War-era posters on the wall behind the bar. Two enormous fan palms in giant black pots at either end of the bar were an attempt to make this a separate space from the crowded dance floor. Hunter ordered a simple bottle of German lager, and then Jodie paid for the drinks on the HARPA credit card.

'What now?' Hunter asked. 'Oh, and can we leave, please?'

Jodie lifted her beer bottle and used it to point. 'The barman says there are some quieter booths up the top.'

'I didn't think there was anything up top,' Hunter said. 'You can't see a damn thing in here. Why do they make these places so bloody dark?'

'Maybe you need glasses,' Jodie said, winking. 'It really has been a long time since you were in a nightclub, hasn't it?'

'Of course it bloody has!' Hunter said. 'The last time I was in a nightclub the bloody Berlin Wall was still up!'

'I knew it!' Jodie said.

'It's right there.' Amy pointed away from the bar and now Hunter squinted through the strange alternating pitch darkness and bright-red laser flashes to see there was an upper level.

Off to the right was a black-painted staircase, and now Amy led the team up the stairs and around to the left where there was a row of half a dozen or so small private booths inside separate Perspex compartments. Each one was covered in 'graffiti', which Jodie explained to Hunter was to lend the place a certain 'street vibe'. Amy swung open the door to the only empty booth, and the small team gathered inside before she closed the door again, shutting the noise out. The bass and drums were now reduced to probably around a third of what they were outside the booth, and Hunter breathed a sigh of relief and drank more lager.

'Well, thank God for that. I don't remember these places being so noisy, hot, or sweaty.'

'I don't know about that,' Toussaint said. 'It reminds me of my youth.'

'But surely, Mentor,' Simeon said, 'you were always studying when you were younger?'

Toussaint put his hand on Simeon's shoulder and gave him a sympathetic smile. 'All I can say now, Simeon, is that all work and no play makes Jacques a dull boy.'

Hunter finally found a reason to smile and chinked bottles with Toussaint.

Amy checked her phone as she had done regularly since Lewis's disappearance in the night back in Cornwall, but there was still nothing. Hunter guessed the young man would call in when he knew more about his son's condition, and until then, they would have to be patient and hope for the best.

'What exactly are we going to do now we're in here?' Jodie asked.

Volkov was staring down through the window at the dance

## 25

After a comfortable night in a decent hotel near the airport, the team made easy progress through the customs at Brandenburg and were soon airborne. Hunter looked outside the Aeroflot passenger jet and saw nothing but an enormous giant rolling ocean of clouds stretching away to the North Pole. His mind turned once again to why Oriax had told Amy to make the trade in Cairo. Before the call, he had expected the trade to take place somewhere in Europe, or at the very least in Israel, where there were various locations connected with the Archangel Michael. Now he turned to Mentor Toussaint and asked him what he made of it.

'I cannot think why Oriax wants to make the trade in Egypt. There are so many sites in the Middle East, including across Egypt – particularly eastern Egypt – but knowing which one Oriax may be heading to is completely impossible to know. I can tell you there's nothing that immediately strikes me as connected with the Archangel Michael in that area of the world.'

'That's what I thought,' Hunter said, scratching his head.

Beside him, Jodie got the attention of the flight attendant who now walked over. The young American ordered an ice-cold can of beer, and Blanco joined her, as did Amy and Volkov. Hunter asked for a bottle of water, as did Simeon, but Toussaint requested a cup of traditional Russian tea.

'I don't think it really matters,' Amy said. She was sitting in front of Hunter and twisted around in her seat so she was able to peer at him through the gap. 'Nachtnebel told us the entire operation is based out of the Rising Star and that that was currently in the train station in Moscow. So we're going to stick to the plan and get to Oriax before the deadline to make the trade in Cairo.'

'If you believe anything that Nachtnebel says,' Jodie said.

'As a matter of fact, I did believe him,' Amy said. 'He said he'd been cut loose by Oriax and wanted to get his revenge. It was the perfect opportunity for him to get that vengeance by setting us on his tail!'

'If they want to do the trade in Cairo,' Blanco said, 'and the train is currently parked up in Moscow, it makes sense that maybe they're going to drive the train south into Egypt. Is that possible?'

'Yes, that is possible,' Toussaint said. 'It is perfectly possible to take a train from Moscow to Cairo and in fact beyond.'

'That is what the bastards are doing,' Volkov said. 'Taking the little train from Moscow to Cairo. That means the hostages must be on board the train!'

'That is exactly what I was thinking,' Simeon said.

'I was kind of hoping that anyway,' Hunter said. 'If I'm being totally honest. I mean... where else would they be? If this Oriax guy likes to live on a train, he's going to want those hostages somewhere close to him, or at least I would if I were a psycho-pathic Illuminati nutcase intent on stealing the Archangel Michael's sword and destroying the world by fulfilling their insane prophecy.'

Hunter caught the eye of the flight attendant who had just delivered his water and now gave her a smile and a wink. 'Just writing the manuscript for a movie.'

She gave him a strange look, turned around and walked back up the cabin.

Jodie and Blanco laughed. Blanco said, 'She looked almost as freaked out as that guy at Brandenburg Airport when I checked in the sword.'

'That was smart saying it was a prop for a movie, though,' Jodie said.

Blanco smiled. 'I thought so.'

Despite the banter, Toussaint and Simeon looked serious and nervous.

'What's the matter, Professor Toussaint?' Hunter asked.

'If only you knew what I know about the sword and the prophecy, then perhaps you would understand the terrible fate that awaits our world if Oriax succeeds in his quest.'

Simeon exchanged a glance with Hunter, then faced the professor. 'Mentor, I have something to ask. It is something that has been on my mind since the beginning of this nightmare and I hope you will not be offended in any way when I ask it.'

Toussaint now lifted his weary old eyes up to his young protégé and gave him an encouraging warm smile. 'Of course, you may ask anything you wish. That is why I am here. That is why I am the mentor.'

'This is the response I had hoped for,' Simeon said. 'You always know what to say.'

'And I also know what you're going to ask as well.'

Simeon's look of concern grew. 'Is it so obvious?'

'It hardly takes a genius given the present circumstances. You are going to ask me if I will share with you the details of the prophecy.'

Hunter now watched as Simeon's expression began to lift and he saw hope in his eyes.

'You are correct, Mentor. That is exactly what I was going to ask you. You're not offended in any way I hope?'

'I am certainly not offended, my young friend. I expected you to ask this question. I expected you would covet this knowledge.'

'I think you'll find we are all coveting that knowledge, Professor Toussaint,' Amy said.

The professor lowered his eyes to the floor, clearly having a quiet internal conversation with himself about the various consequences of what he was about to say, but none of it made any difference. These good people who were fighting alongside him against Oriax and his small army deserved to know. More than that, they needed to know. Their lives could depend on it.

'Then come with me to the back of the aircraft. We might be able to get some privacy in the galley for a few moments.'

The team rose from their seats and followed Toussaint to the rear galley, which was mercifully free of flight attendants – at least for now.

'What I am about to say may sound mad, but it is true. At least, I believe it is true, and I think you all will, too.'

The plane continued northeast through the cold northern sky like sharpened steel slicing through silk. Time seemed to slow down. The professor now brushed away some invisible dust from his trousers and the cabin swayed gently from side to side in response to some turbulence. The HARPA team, Volkov and Simeon closed in around Toussaint, their faces muted in the soft light of the plane's interior.

'The prophecy was never written down,' the professor began, his voice low and even and entirely without emotion. It seemed to Hunter that this ancient secret may well have been a terrible burden for the old man, and unloading it today was coming as a relief.

'They were very careful never to write it down, never on any papyrus or parchment, it was never put in any book and hidden away in a church or a monastery. It passed as a spoken tradition from one mentor to the next across the centuries, but as time faded, the terrible meaning of the prophecy stayed as alive and real as ever.'

The plane shuddered once again as it ploughed through more turbulence, shaking the cups and glasses in the galley and making them rattle. The professor never responded or paused, but continued his story.

'But not everyone agreed that this was the best way. Several centuries ago there was a division in the Guild and for a time there was great upheaval and arguments about not only how the prophecy would be handed down, but also other doctrinal disputes, specifically about the true meaning of the prophecy, and how it could be interpreted. Some even argued that the angel who spoke the prophecy was not the Archangel Michael, but Lucifer.'

'Holy crap,' Jodie said. 'Is that true?'

'No, and not many ever believed so, not even the League of St Michael.'

'The League, Mentor?' Simeon asked.

Toussaint smiled now. 'We're coming to that. In the end, no resolution could be found to these disagreements and the Guild broke into two. The one as you know it today, the one of which I am Mentor, continued the tradition of passing the prophecy by spoken word, while a splinter group formed and began to document everything with the written word. They called themselves the League of St Michael.'

'I think things are beginning to come together,' Amy said.

'I agree,' Simeon said. 'Now I think I too am beginning to understand.'

Toussaint nodded. 'And things will only get clearer.'

'They would be fully clear if you would tell us the prophecy,' Jodie mumbled.

Toussaint nodded. 'Very well. The prophecy – or more properly referred to as the Angel Prophecy – is this: "He who wields the flaming sword will inherit the power of God".'

'So whoever has the sword will have divine power?' Hunter asked.

Toussaint nodded glumly. 'I believe so. Now you see why Oriax must be stopped. No one man can wield that sort of power.'

'Oriax hasn't got the sword yet, Professor,' Amy said, reassuring him.

'And he's not going to get it, either,' Hunter put in.

'Amen to that,' Blanco said.

'That is all very well to say,' Toussaint said. 'But the Illuminati is a powerful organisation. We are but just a handful of people. And you have already now learned the truth about the Guild of St Michael. We are a very small organisation and very poorly funded. In our hearts the fight is strong, but we cannot muster any real power to go up against a group as large as the Illuminati. I am very worried that they will crush us at the final turn, and not only kill all of your friends and colleagues but also take the sword forever.'

'We're not going to let that happen, Professor,' Amy said.

'No, and neither will I!' Simeon said. 'I will give my life in the service of the Guild, and I will destroy as many of those bastards as I can before I die! We can destroy them all!'

'*Calme-toi, mon fils,*' Toussaint said. 'Calm down.'

Hunter admired and appreciated Simeon's enthusiasm, but knowing what he now knew about the true nature of the Guild of

St Michael, which most charitably could be described as an amateur organisation, he felt the young Frenchman was being slightly naïve in his approach to the upcoming showdown with the Illuminati.

The truth was that Hunter doubted even the HARPA team's ability to take on a man such as Oriax and his organisation, but he was going to make a damn good try of it.

## 26

Hunter was not impressed by the façade of Kursky railway station, which resembled a modest regional airport. Other stations he had visited in Russia had beautifully ornate architectural motifs which reflected traditional Russian style in a subtle yet commanding way. Other parts of the station were even worse, reminding him of a modern Western shopping mall or some kind of international airport, with its modular shops built into a giant cube of polished stone, chrome and glass. These were the parts of the railway station that could have been anywhere on Earth and reflected no culture at all. The only thing a place like this reflected was the commercialisation of life itself. This was why Hunter spent most of his life immersed in antiquity.

He had forgotten to set his watch to local time back on the plane, so now he rolled it forward an hour and was delighted to see it was suddenly lunchtime, but that would have to wait.

He followed Amy across to the ticket office where she bought the required number of tickets to get the entire team through to the relevant platform, which was the platform furthest from the station, requiring them to take an underground pedestrianised tunnel to their destination. The small group now made their way through the tunnel until they reached some steps. Stepping up onto the platform, Hunter saw mostly commuter trains, emblazoned with various designs such as red stars, but the Rising Star was a very different kettle of fish. It was an enormous, ugly 1970s locomotive painted entirely black, and every carriage was the same uniform corrugated chrome. The diesel engines were running and he could smell the exhaust fumes wafting over the platform from time to time as the breeze blew them down in their direction. Luckily there were other people on the platform boarding a train on the opposite side, so they were able to blend in while they took stock of the situation and studied the best way to get on board Oriax's train.

Looking down the far end of the platform towards the end of the train, Hunter saw men in coats and beanies loading crates into the Rising Star's rearmost carriage. He pointed them out to Amy.

'That must be the food and water going in down there at the back,' he said.

She agreed. 'You think that's our best way in?'

'I think it's got to be, hasn't it?'

Volkov walked over to the men with his hands in his pockets and meandered around in the crowd. He came back a few minutes later. 'I overheard the men talking. They are going immediately to Egypt and think they can make the journey of a little over three thousand kilometres in around twenty hours. The Rising Star has a top speed of two hundred kilometres per hour.'

'Did they talk about the route?' Amy asked.

'They said it goes down through Russia, south into Georgia, across Turkey, through Syria, Lebanon, Israel, Jordan and then turns into Egypt where it will stop.'

'Then we need to make plans to get on board that train as fast as possible,' Hunter said.

'Agreed,' said Amy. 'If that thing gets away without us on it we're never going to see our friends again. Not unless someone around here can drive their own train and catch up with it?'

'I wouldn't mind giving that a go,' Jodie said, staring at the locomotive. 'I bet it's a bitch to stop from high speed.'

'That's right,' Hunter said. 'You're a bit of a speed freak, aren't you?'

'No one's stealing any trains and going for joyrides today,' Amy said. 'We've got to get into the back of this train and when we're on board we can search each carriage one by one until we find our friends. We take the sword in case we screw up and need to hand it over to save them.'

'I don't think it's a great idea to take the sword on board the train,' Blanco said. 'I hear what you say about needing it at hand if anything goes wrong and we're forced to hand it over to save Quinn's life and the lives of the rest of our friends, but to me, it just seems too risky.'

'We need to take it with us. You can't stay behind here in Moscow.'

'It's too risky,' Blanco repeated. 'Oriax could get the sword if I come with you.'

Amy shook her head and replied to him, her voice defiant. 'I would never let Oriax get his hands on the sword.'

Toussaint solemnly nodded. 'He can never get his hands on it.'

'But we just don't know what's going to happen from here on in with the mission,' Amy said. 'If things go badly and it comes down to a choice between saving the lives of our friends and handing the sword over to Oriax, then you know what I'm going to do every time.'

Blanco nodded in agreement. 'I feel the same way, Amy. I would hand over the sword even to a psychopath like Oriax if it meant saving Quinn's life.'

'That's why it's coming with us,' Amy said. 'I know it's a gamble, but that's a chance I'm prepared to take because I won't let Quinn die, not under any circumstances. It's decided.'

'Well, you are the leader of the HARPA team in the absence of Jim,' Blanco said.

'You're damn right I am,' Amy said. 'So now let's find a way to get on that train!'

_____

## 27

'Keep your heads down, everyone. Look Russian,' Hunter said.

The English archaeologist, who to say had been out of his depth on this mission was the understatement of the century, now walked alongside Volkov, Amy, and Jodie with the others walking a yard or two behind as they made their way slowly through the crowd on the platform towards the very far end of the Rising Star. It was a little quieter down here, but the men loading the crates and boxes onto the rear carriage paid them no attention. It was hard, busy work as they walked backwards and forwards from a large pile of inventory stacked up at the very end of the platform.

'Look Russian, you say,' Volkov said. 'Is not funny.'

Ignoring his comment, Hunter turned to Volkov. 'I don't think there's going to be a pretty way to do this.'

The Russian agreed. Without further word to Hunter or anyone else on the team, Volkov now walked up to one of the men who was holding a clipboard and ticking off each crate as it went onto the train. Hunter listened to him talking to the man in

Russian, but could not understand a word. He had no trouble understanding what Volkov did next, which was to tear the clip-board from the man and ram it sideways into his throat, smashing his windpipe and causing him to stagger back off the platform. He tried to reach for the end of the train to try to stop himself from falling, missed and crashed down off the platform behind the train onto the tracks, never to be seen or heard of again.

'Is no more problem,' Volkov said.

The other two men of the three-man crew who had been working at the back of the train now reacted, not like lightning but slowly and with confusion. Hunter deduced that they were not regular members of Oriax's crew, but merely hired labourers possibly even working for the station. One of them began berating Volkov as he stepped around and stared down at the man who was lying out of Hunter's view on the tracks, pointing at him and then turning back to Volkov with animated hand gestures, shouting and presumably swearing. The other man took a different approach and now pulled a mobile phone from his pocket and started to make a call. HARPA sprang into action. Hunter went to the man with the phone, twisted it out of his hand and punched him in the face, knocking him back into a large open crate of citrus fruits. He hit him two more times until he was knocked out, while Jodie walked to the man who was shouting and swearing and kneed him in the groin. As he tumbled forward clutching between his legs, Jodie brought her booted thigh up and kneed him in the face, knocking him back down on the tracks beside his friend, unconscious.

'That was amazing!' Simeon said.

Toussaint shook his head and made the sign of the cross. 'May God forgive me for being a party to such violence and killing.'

'I don't think any of them are actually dead, Professor,' Amy said. 'Now, everyone, get on the train!'

Hunter and the rest of the team now filed into the rear carriage, closed the door and found themselves in a neatly ordered storeroom with a freezer compartment on one wall filled with frozen food, ice cream, and frozen meats. On the other side were cupboards full of dried goods, wide open as they were still being loaded up by the men who were now unconscious. Pasta, rice, tinned beans, tinned vegetables, large bags of potatoes, and copious amounts of vodka as well as other alcoholic spirits, wines and beers were all stacked up ready for the journey. There was also a section full of fresh fruits and vegetables, presumably where the citrus fruits outside had been heading – lemons, limes oranges, apples, pears, cabbages, broccoli and carrots.

'This place looks like a bloody supermarket,' Hunter said.

'Only the very best for the head of the Illuminati,' Volkov said. 'Meanwhile, thanks to inflation, normal families struggle to feed themselves with even the most basic ingredients. Is not funny.'

Hunter saw Volkov was genuinely upset by the ostentatious display of so many kinds of food and drink that had been imported from all over the world to supply one man and his small team of followers. He did not doubt though that Volkov would soon have an opportunity for revenge. Before Amy could brief the team on the next phase of the rescue operation, they all felt the carriage jerk forward, spilling some of the food onto the floor.

'Looks like we're on the move!' Amy said.

'We need to get started looking for our friends,' Hunter said. 'I recommend Blanco keeps the sword back here, out of sight. I also recommend that Professor Toussaint and Simeon stay behind with him to help defend it.'

'No, this is unacceptable!' Simeon said. 'I deserve a chance to kill Oriax and his evil force!'

Before Hunter could speak, Toussaint reached out and put his hand on Simeon's shoulder.

'My son, you will have many opportunities to serve the Guild in the future. I think you should listen to what Dr Hunter says and stay behind. We need someone to defend us here and I don't think you are ready to fight the Illuminati yet.'

Hunter could see Simeon had been revving up to have a go at him and defy his orders, but when Toussaint spoke he folded like a deck chair, nodded his head and explained to everyone that he would stay behind to help Sal Blanco guard the mentor, and the sword.

'This would be the greatest honour of all my life,' Simeon said. 'To protect the Sword of the Archangel Michael itself from this evil!'

Hunter wasn't certain if Simeon had decided to stay behind without a fight because of a genuine desire to defend the sword and protect Professor Toussaint, or it was because his inexperience in fighting had caused him to lose his nerve at the final hurdle. Hunter didn't care what the motivation was; he was happy that he had agreed to stay behind to help Blanco protect the sword and the professor all the same. While the young French Guild member might not be experienced enough to engage in a full-scale firefight or hand-to-hand combat further up the train, Hunter was satisfied he could defend the rear carriage, at least for as long as it took for backup to arrive.

'Then we're all settled,' Hunter said. 'Let's get moving up the train. Our priority is to disarm these guys and take their weapons. Right now we're armed with nothing more than knives out of this kitchen and Volkov's handgun. Talking of which, how did you get through German and Russian customs?'

'Is not relevant.'

Hunter shrugged, guessing Babineaux had a very long reach.

'I agree with Max,' Amy said. 'We're gonna need some more weapons.'

'Sure, but we're not going to find them back here,' Jodie said. 'So let's get our asses up there and find Quinn!'

## 28

Hunter didn't have to wait very long for an opportunity to disarm someone. After they left the store carriage in the back of the train, the next carriage along was another storeroom, this time some sort of laundry. There were washing machines, tumble dryers, and cupboards stacked with fresh sheets, flannels and toilet rolls. He was reaching the end of this carriage when the door opened and revealed a man wearing a set of shabby white work clothes. Hunter thought he was clearly on his way to start washing Oriax's underwear. He paused in the doorway, freezing for a second like a rabbit in some headlights, and fixed his eyes on Hunter. The moment seemed to last forever, but then he staggered back out of the door, slamming it shut behind him.

The train was moving much faster now, and as Hunter swayed from side to side inside the carriage, he tried to retain his composure and turned to the rest of the team, who had all seen the man.

'We need to get after him before he raises the alarm,' Hunter said.

Hunter raced forward and was reaching out for the door when it opened once again. He never hesitated, and instinctively slammed it back into the frame as hard as he could. He heard a crunching sound and a muffled thud and then opened the door to see the man in white on the floor, unconscious from the door striking his head. Standing above him was another man, this time dressed in black, whom Hunter recognised as one of the goons they'd fought in the Berlin nightclub. This time, the man was armed with a handgun, which he was already holding in his right hand, and he now lifted it and fired.

Hunter cried out for everyone to hit the deck and take cover, which they all instantly obeyed, letting the man's bullet race across the carriage and strike the door at the far end. Hunter leapt to his feet and charged through the open doorway. He had considered slamming the door again but that would only allow Oriax to send more men down the train. The man fired a second time as Hunter was in mid-air but fired too high and missed, and the bullet ricocheted off the carriage wall just as Hunter rugby-tackled the man to the ground, slamming his head down against the floor of the train carriage and reaching down for his gun. He twisted the weapon out of his hand and then brought it up and struck him on his temple with its grip, knocking him out. He waved the gun in the air.

'Now we've got two guns! Everyone forward!'

He climbed up off the man and the team raced through the third carriage, which this time was a simple dining car and bar, but Hunter got the impression this was not where Oriax enjoyed his meals. This was the place where Oriax's guards and minions gathered at the end of a hard day's Illuminati service. It was neat and tidy, but basic and showed no signs of opulence or luxury whatsoever. He carried on through this carriage and into the next one, which was a passenger carriage filled with seats. At the far end, he saw an apparatus on the ceiling which seemed to incorporate a roller blind. This was the cinema that Volkov had told them about.

'Oriax really does think of everything!'

'Oriax is a bastard who's going to eat my fist,' Volkov said.

'Fair enough,' Hunter said with a shrug and carried on into the next carriage. This time they were met with stiff resistance. The carriage looked like Oriax's private salon – there was a large oak table on one side of the carriage and bookcases on the other. Filing cabinets lined the opposite wall, and at the far end, a grand piano was bolted to the floor. Behind the grand piano was a door leading into the study, and now Hunter watched in horror as at least half a dozen men streamed through the door with compact machine pistols and began raking the hell out of their end of the carriage.

'Back! Back… back!' Hunter screamed.

Luckily only he and Volkov had stepped into the salon, and everyone else had remained in the cinema carriage. Hunter and Volkov took cover behind the filing cabinets and desk and returned fire. The men were good but slightly impetuous and overzealous in their actions, especially in the aiming department, preferring the 'shoot everything in sight' method. Both Hunter and Volkov understood the limitations of this approach, namely that they would run out of ammunition soon and all at the same time. This happened moments later, and Hunter and Volkov returned fire. Hunter fired ahead of him off to the left, while Volkov took the men on the right. Some of Volkov's rounds punched into the grand piano, splintering the wood and in one case breaking one of the strings, which now twanged wildly, producing a rumbling low E flat throughout the carriage. The Russian's other rounds hit their mark and killed two of the men. Hunter was more successful, shooting three of the men while they reloaded, which left only one defending Oriax. He now smacked his new magazine into the weapon's receiver and, walking backwards towards the door to make a retreat, he sprayed his gun from side to side. Hunter and Volkov merely ducked down behind their respective cover positions and let the bullets wash over them. Hunter had been in genuine active battlefield situations and remained calm, as did Volkov.

When the new magazine had run out, they both darted up from their cover positions and fired on the man again, but he had already slithered away into the next carriage.

'Advance!' Volkov screamed. 'Everyone, advance on enemy!'

Hunter and Volkov led the charge through the salon, skirting the desk and then the grand piano before stepping through the door at the end. Hunter had expected to see the man fleeing back to base to report the massacre of the men in the study, but instead, he was dumbfounded when he saw they had fallen for the oldest trick in the book. The men Oriax had sent forward were nothing more than a feint, mere bait to draw Hunter, Volkov and the rest of the team forward. Standing in the carriage, which was decorated with sumptuous leather-studded furniture with gold-painted woodwork and even boasted a chandelier hanging down from the ceiling, was a man in a very expensive suit, surrounded by at least half a dozen men holding MP5 compact machine guns.

'What do you think, Dr Hunter?' the man said. 'Do you think your two handguns are a match for these six compact machine pistols?'

Hunter and Volkov exchanged a look of despair, and both dropped their guns without being asked. Amy quickly appeared behind Hunter with the rest of the team a few steps in tow. She looked at Hunter, equally as frustrated and full of fear as Volkov had just done.

'My God, Oriax... is that you?' Amy asked.

He nodded. 'Yes, I am Oriax, although this is obviously not my real name. I am Aleksey Petkevich, from Minsk in Belarus... and you are now my prisoners. Step away from your weapons.' He turned to his right where a tall, noble-looking man was standing. 'Jophiel, go and get those guns. We don't want any nasty surprises.'

'At once,' Jophiel said.

Hunter and the others waited on high alert as the man took their guns away and returned to Petkevich.

'Now search them all!'

## 29

Hunter reluctantly allowed Jophiel to search him for weapons, as did the others. Then he raised his hands again. Beside him, the large Russian did the same and they were followed by the rest of the team. Petkevich now ordered everyone to take a seat where they were standing at the end of the carriage and then requested that Hunter and Amy come forward to other end of the carriage, where there was a privately arranged corner lounge suite of crushed purple velvet decorated with gold tassels. Hunter restrained himself from making a comment about the décor, owing largely to the six men armed with compact machine pistols standing a few yards to his right. Instead, he took a seat on the chair, which in fairness was one of the most comfortable he had ever sat on, as did Amy, and then finally Petkevich joined them with an aristocratic flourish.

Petkevich clapped his hands together with joy as he reclined in the seat.

'It is so wonderful to find you both here on my train! Surely you did not believe I would trust you when you told me you would deliver the sword? No, I'm sure you did not think that. So I have men out all over Europe searching for you and yet here you are. You are so polite that you actually came to me and saved me any further bother. I am presuming that the sword is also on board my train?'

Hunter and Amy hesitated for one second too long.

'But of course it is!' Petkevich said smugly. 'Of course it is – because you calculated that you needed the sword to release your friends and if you came here today without the sword and things went wrong – you could call what has happened here today "going wrong", I think – you thought you would be able to use the sword as some kind of bartering chip?'

'Maybe that's what we do think!' Amy said. Hunter heard the frustration and anger in her voice. 'Maybe I told my teammate to damage or bend the sword as much as he could if we didn't come back by a certain time?'

Hunter thought it was a weak gambit, and by the uproarious laughter of Aleksey Petkevich, so did he. 'Come now, Agent Fox! Surely you do not expect me to believe this? You have here Dr Hunter, one of the United Nations' finest archaeologists. He is, I believe, a senior researcher at UNESCO. I know this because I have his superior, Professor Juliette Bonnaire, as a guest here on this very train. You really expect me to believe a man like this would agree to you damaging the sword of the Archangel Michael just because I caught you?'

He leaned forward and slapped his knee, descending once again into uncontrollable laughter, and now the men with the machine guns joined in the fun.

While Petkevich was talking, Hunter scanned the carriage for anything he could use as a weapon, or how easily they could get away if trouble broke out, but there was no hope of anything like that. Just one MP5 would be enough to kill him and everyone else on his team should Petkevich order it, which Hunter was absolutely certain he would do if Petkevich thought his safety was in any serious jeopardy.

'No! No... no,' Petkevich continued. 'I don't think that is what you have planned at all. I think you brought the sword because you wanted to use it to bargain for your friends' lives but only if things went wrong. I think you planned to make some sort of idle threat like you have just done. I think the real reason you brought the sword was because you thought you would overcome me and my men and then you would hand it over to the pathetic Guild of St Michael that you have allied yourself with and this will be your little adventure over. Sadly, that is not how things have worked out. But what is it that you say? That is how the biscuit breaks!'

Amy tensed her jaw. 'I would say that's how the cookie crumbles because I'm American.'

He slapped his knee again. 'Indeed you are American, yes. But I am Belarusian so I think I will say that is how the biscuit breaks. And whether we talk about biscuits or cookies, or breaking or crumbling, the fact remains you have lost here today! Your arrogance has led you to come to my very inner sanctum and bring the sword here! Such is your hubris that you think you can overcome me and win. Your plan has been a total failure.' He waved these last words away as if he was dismissing her out of the carriage.

'You're one to talk about hubris,' Hunter said.

Petkevich now swivelled his eyes to the English archaeologist. 'You have something to say, Dr Hunter?'

'All this,' Hunter said, gesturing at the carriage with a sweeping palm. 'All this tacky nonsense. You drive up and down on a train because you're too scared to stay in the same place for longer than a night. You sitting here talking about how we failed, as if the fat lady has sung. And this purple velvet chair, damn it.'

'But it is over!' Petkevich said. 'You have lost. And now you are my prisoners, but perhaps we could call you guests. Yes, perhaps I should call you guests – after all, that is how I have come to see your compatriots. That is how I have come to see Jim Gates and his lovely darling wife Susanna. That is how I have come to see Professor Juliette Bonnaire of UNESCO. That is also how I have come to see agent Quinn Mosley, your very own teammate.'

'You better not have hurt Quinn!' Amy said. 'I'm a patient woman and I can tolerate all kinds of things, but the one thing I won't stand for is any of my team members being hurt or intimidated in any way!'

'And what makes you think I have hurt her?' Petkevich leaned forward now, drawing closer to Amy as if they were enjoying a simple conversation between friends. 'As soon as I kidnapped Quinn Mosley, she became – how can I put this – my asset. And I am not the kind of person who would not look after his own assets. In fact, I have taken the very greatest care of all of my assets across my life. Why would Quinn Mosley be any different?'

Hunter felt a sense of rage the way Petkevich was talking about Quinn and the others he had snatched so brutally. But he could see that Amy was barely able to control her anger and for exactly the same reason.

'You are an asshole, Petkevich,' Amy said. 'Quinn Mosley is not an asset, she is a human being, and so are Jim and Susanna Gates and Juliette Bonnaire. You snatched them out of their lives as if they were nothing more than pawns in your disgusting little game... whatever the hell kind of game you're playing.'

Petkevich laughed again, seemingly untouchable by anything they could say to him. 'That is a very brave and noble speech,

Agent Fox, but I'm afraid I have heard it all before. And I will dismiss you as I have dismissed everyone in my past who has ever spoken to me like this. Many people who have used that tone with me have ended up dead. You can count yourself lucky that for now you are allowed to live.'

'You talk about killing people as if it's some kind of sport or hobby,' Amy said with barely concealed contempt. 'You disgust me.'

Petkevich casually shrugged. 'It's more of a business transaction than either of those things, but there it is. Every single person I have ever killed has deserved to die, and who are you to decide where I should set my moral compass? No doubt you represent and support the same disgusting vile debauchery that your government represents. Why would I take a lecture on morality or ethics from a person like you? It makes my skin crawl to think of the things you believe in and support.'

'You don't know what I believe in,' Amy said.

Hunter glanced down at the end of the carriage and saw Jodie and Volkov. Volkov was hard to read, but it wasn't difficult for him to see the emotion on Jodie's face. She was working hard to stay in control but he recognised a look of typical defiance in her eyes. If anyone was going to go down fighting all the way to the bottom, that person was Jodie Priest.

'I don't really care what you think you believe in,' Petkevich continued. 'Your entire culture is as rotten as a stinking mould-covered apple at the bottom of a barrel somewhere. And you have lost here today, which is a good thing. It shows me the Lord is listening and fighting alongside me to rid the world of filth like you and your disgusting ideas.'

Hunter looked outside the train window at a flat agricultural landscape almost devoid of all features racing past in a blur. He wondered exactly what this man and his goons had in store for him and the others. Would they be murdered before the train got to Egypt? Why was the train going to Egypt? Were Quinn and Jim and Susanna Gates also on board the train along with Juliette? His thoughts were interrupted by a crashing sound at the far end of the carriage, and he turned to see the man Petkevich had called Jophiel marching Simeon, Toussaint and Blanco at gunpoint into the carriage to join Volkov and Jodie. Another man was standing behind Jophiel, carrying Blanco's backpack, and Hunter saw the handle of the sword sticking out of it and felt a wave of crushing defeat wash over him. Blanco gave him an apologetic shrug, but Hunter felt no blame was attached to his old friend from New York.

'Ah, the sword arrives at last,' Petkevich said, rising from his seat. 'Bring it here, Jophiel! I want to see it at last.'

The fear of failure hit Hunter like a ton of bricks as the man called Jophiel pulled the sword out of the bag, walked it up the carriage, handing it to Petkevich. Now he watched the Belarusian's eyes greedily survey his conquest as he held it in his hands, mere inches from his eyes, so close it looked like he was almost sniffing the steel.

'Yes, it is mine at last! Finally, I will secure my divine destiny! No one can stop me now, not if I hold the very power of God in my hand.'

He studied it closely for a few moments, almost as if he was an antique expert trying to find some flaw with it to knock its value down, but then he beamed broadly, first at the sword itself and then at Jophiel.

'When did you learn about the prophecy, Petkevich?' Amy asked.

His eyes darted up from the sword to Amy. 'I first learnt of it when I stumbled across some strange passages in the writings of an old monk who lived at the Zhyrovichy Monastery in the north-west of Belarus, my homeland.'

'Was that something you read as part of a course or just for fun on a beach?' Hunter said.

Petkevich ignored him. 'Uladzimir was a great scholar and a devout believer, a believer of something greater than himself, greater than all of us. I doubt people like you could understand such a man.'

'But how did he learn of the prophecy?' Amy asked. 'Did he know about the League of St Michael?'

Petkevich laughed. 'Did he know about it? Ha! Uladzimir was in the League. He was the final mentor of the League! But towards the end of his life, his studies made him change his mind about the necessity to write the prophecy down, and he made the decision not to pass them on to anyone else in the League and to destroy all written references to it, including his own life's work, but he overlooked a few tattered old pages of one of his early manuscripts. It was this that I eventually found in the crypt of his monastery. After I read it, I knew at once it was my destiny! The wielder of the flaming sword will have the power of God! After this, I dedicated every moment of my life to finding the sword!'

'Focused yet humble,' Hunter muttered.

Petkevich scowled at him, then turned to Jophiel, handing him the sword. 'Take this and put it in my safe. We will take it out again when we're at our destination.'

Jophiel took the sword and walked back to the rear of the carriage, disappearing out of sight.

'You see, you cannot possibly win now,' Petkevich said. 'You have failed and I have won. I am holding on the Rising Star all of your friends hostage, I am holding you hostage and now I have the sword which is my rightful destiny. I will fulfil the prophecy!' Petkevich's face broke into a depraved, wicked smile and he recited the prophecy for all to hear. 'He who puts the flaming sword to the flame of fire will inherit the power of God!'

When Hunter heard Petkevich say the prophecy, something instantly bothered him, but he couldn't put his finger on what it was. Before he had a chance to think about it, Amy spoke up.

'So what are you going to do with us now?' she said.

'You are going to be taken to your private quarters where you'll be locked in and you will stay until we arrive at our final destination.'

'You're going to keep us locked in sleeping compartments until we get to Cairo?' Hunter asked. 'We need to travel through half of the Middle East before then! It's going to take nearly a day!'

Petkevich nodded. 'Yes, it will indeed take nearly a day. My train is very fast at two hundred kilometres per hour, but it is a very long way.'

'And what were you going to do with us once we get to Cairo?' Amy asked. 'You wanted to make the trade with us at the pyramids?'

'My plan was simple. You would go to the pyramids to conduct the trade in good faith, and Jophiel and my other men would meet you there, take the sword, and kill you. Then the rest of the hostages would be killed.'

'So why not just kill us now?' Amy asked.

Petkevich looked at her like she was mad. 'Because I have a better idea! You will now be the first people I kill with the sword!'

Hunter leant into her and whispered. 'You had to ask, didn't you?'

'Enough of this!' Petkevich turned to a man behind him. 'Take them to their compartments and lock them in!'

Hunter felt a man grab him by the shoulders and pull him up out of his chair. Someone else did the same to Amy, and other goons swarmed around the rest of the team at the back of the carriage. The next thing Hunter knew, he was being marched through the carriage door and taken into a carriage with a side corridor and private compartments on their right. A man with a machine pistol broke the group up into twos and then locked each couple up inside a private compartment. Hunter and Amy, who had been paired together in the furthest carriage, now stared at one another almost unable to believe what had happened.

'Well, that went well,' Hunter said.

Amy shrugged. 'Hey... try to look on the bright side.'

'What? That we're getting a free ride across the Middle East?'

'No!' Amy said. 'Petkevich said that everyone else he is holding hostage is right here on board the Rising Star! That's great news, can't you see? And we're here too so we're all together at last!'

'Yes, but the problem is that we're not together, are we? Not only has our own team been completely split up and locked in separate compartments, but we have no idea whereabouts on the train Quinn and the others are either. And we've all been disarmed. And Petkevich knows we're here so we lack the element of surprise. Oh yeah, and they've all got machine guns. And the sword.'

'God, you're such a glass-half-empty kind of guy,' Amy said.

Hunter couldn't help but smile at the American woman, and he walked over to her now and gave her a long, tight hug. They kissed for a long time and then sat down opposite each other on soft chairs by the window. A thin mist hung in a flat white sheet across the plains they were now racing through, but it was still largely open countryside with few features. Hunter knew his geography very well and he supposed in the hour or so they had already been on board the train, they would have done probably a little over two hundred kilometres and would be slowly making their way to Voronezh. It was a long journey south through the Caucuses towards Georgia, Turkey and eventually the Middle East. At least he had some good company for that time.

'I'm sorry,' he said. 'I'm just so out of my depth on this mission. I lost my temper so just ignore my sarcasm. I was born with it.'

'It's fine, forget about it. I feel the same way, Max. We worked out right from the very beginning that this mission was going to be completely different to everything else we've ever done together. We were right there when we said that our normal skills were better suited to tracking down ancient relics or sites of antiquity. This time everything was different, we were thrown off our game. Not only were we being asked to play by a completely different set of rules, but the one person we needed most to help us out was Quinn and she wasn't working alongside us because she was the mission.'

'Exactly. I'm sorry if I haven't been at my best, but I'm an archaeologist, Amy, and all of our previous missions have required my skills to help us get to the bottom of things and complete the mission successfully. Before HARPA, I spent most of my time dealing with the ancient world, the classical world, pottery, artefacts, and relics. You can even throw some clues and symbols in there and I'll have a go at it, but for some reason this mission really got to me...'

'I think you're doing just great,' Amy said. 'We're all out of our league on this one, Max. But we're doing it because of how we feel about our teammates. I'm so proud of us, the way we stepped up and risked our lives to save them. We're not going to fail. So you just pull yourself together and get that chin up, mister!'

Hunter was very glad he had met Amy Fox, and now he felt that more than ever. They reached out and hugged, and then started kissing again. Hunter pulled away from her and stepped over to the locked door where he pulled down the blinds.

'What are you doing?' Amy asked.

'Just giving us a little privacy.'

'Why? Are you going to try to escape?'

'Not exactly,' Hunter said, then he stepped over to Amy with a devilish grin. 'You heard Mr Petkevich – we do have twenty hours to ourselves.'

## 30

Hunter was awoken by the sound of squealing brakes and then a hard jolt as the carriage came to a sudden stop. The Rising Star had finally come to the end of its journey and had woken both him and Amy up. He was a little dazed and confused, having spent most of the previous twenty hours lying on the pull-out bed in their sleeping compartment. Now he rubbed his eyes and tried to wake himself up to take in the beautiful joys of a Cairo morning.

'And how is the ancient city of Cairo today?' he asked Amy. 'I've been to the Ramses train station more times than I can remember. You know it was built back in 1892, at least the one you're looking at out there right now. They usually describe it as a miracle marriage of modern engineering and ancient Islamic aesthetics... Would you agree?'

'Yeah... we're not in Cairo.'

Hunter dragged himself up to his elbows and squinted at Amy, who was now sitting on the side of the bed and staring out of the window. She too looked sleepy and confused, but he didn't doubt what she had just said.

'We're not in Cairo?'

'That's what I said, Max. There's nothing wrong with your hearing.'

Hunter swivelled around beside her and now squinted even more as he stared out of the carriage window at the view beyond. 'Bugger me, that really is not Cairo.'

'But where the hell is it?'

Hunter felt a chill go up his spine as he stared outside. 'I think I might know.'

'What do you mean? It's just desert mountains.'

'It's sandstone massifs, the type common to the southern Sinai. I think we're at Aqaba.'

'Oh, I always wanted to come here,' she said, her face turning into a frustrated frown. 'Where the hell is Aqaba, Max?'

'I already said – southern Sinai. I think I know where our host is taking us. Do you remember when he quoted the prophecy?'

'Kinda. Remind me.'

'He said, "He who puts the flaming sword to the flame of fire will inherit the power of God".'

Amy's face lit up. 'Which is different from what Toussaint told us!'

'Exactly. Toussaint said, "He who wields the flaming sword will inherit the power of God." That's a small but important distinction that tells us where we're going. Damn it, I should have been on this earlier.' Hunter smacked his forehead with the palm of his hand. 'Bugger it.'

Amy gave him a withering look. 'Feel better?'

'No, I feel exactly like before but now I have a sore head.'

She leaned forward and kissed him. 'Better?'

'Not really, but maybe some more of that and I might be.'

She pulled back. 'Where are we going, Max?'

He blew out a breath. 'Not sure really. After Avril I kind of decided against serious relationships, but—'

'Not us, you fool,' she said with a knowing smirk. 'I know where we're going. I meant where are we going today?'

'It's all in the reference to the "flame of fire",' he said, 'which means—' They heard the door being unlocked and then it swung open, to reveal Jophiel.

'Time to leave!' he said. He made his point a little clearer by waving a handgun in their faces. 'We need to take a new ride.'

'And what if we refuse?' Amy asked.

'Please don't make this more difficult than it has to be. Just leave the train!'

Hunter and Amy looked at one another and knew they had no choice but to comply. They both stopped to pull on some clothes over their underwear and then they followed Jophiel out of their compartment and along the corridor to the end where the carriage's external door was already open. Hunter felt a familiar wave of hot, dry air blowing through his hair. Having been in many deserts in this part of the world during his time as an archaeologist and before that as an officer in the army, he knew the feeling very well. He looked up at the hot blue sky and wished he had a hat. They stepped down off the carriage to find the rest of their team, plus Toussaint, Simeon and Blanco, standing out in the desert sun on a sun-drenched railway platform.

'Quinn!' Amy cried out.

Hunter watched as the American FBI agent ran down the platform and embraced her young protégé. Now he saw Jim Gates and his wife, Susanna, just behind a gaggle of Petkevich's men. Finally, he saw his boss at UNESCO, Professor Juliette Bonnaire. She too was slightly obscured by the heavily armed men in black lurking around Petkevich.

Hunter strolled over to the small group and gave Juliette Bonnaire a brief embrace and they kissed each other on the cheek. She looked up at him, and he saw tears had reddened her eyes. Now she smiled and clamped his head in her hands, thanking him profusely in French for rescuing her. 'I knew you would not forget me, *mon chiot...*' she said.

'*De rien*,' Hunter said. 'I'm just glad you're safe. I'm glad you're all safe.'

Hunter looked around the hot dusty platform as the entire team greeted each other; some with tears, others a little more stoically. He counted eleven of them now – him, Amy, Blanco, Jodie, Quinn, Jim and Susanna Gates, Professor Juliette Bonnaire, Volkov, Simeon and Toussaint. It was beginning to be quite a force if they could organise themselves and get weapons.

Petkevich now broke through his circle of heavily armed men and stepped forward to speak to Hunter and Amy.

'Welcome to Aqaba!' he said.

'Aqaba?' Jodie asked. 'Where is that?'

'The Aqaba governorate is in southern Israel,' Hunter said, looking at Petkevich. 'So, we're really not going to Cairo then?'

Petkevich laughed. 'Why, do you doubt me?'

'I would believe a worm-like Nachtnebel over you,' Amy said.

'You make me laugh, Agent Fox!' Petkevich said. 'It is just too bad that I am going to have to kill you at the end of this mission – and please don't speak badly of the dead.'

'You killed Nachtnebel?'

'No, he signed his own death warrant when he betrayed me. My people in Germany dispatched him a few hours ago with a garotte. You on the other hand will have a far more glorious death, as I have already said.'

'Why not just do it now? Are you a coward?' Amy asked.

Hunter reached out and touched her arm. 'Steady on, darling. There's no need to be silly.'

'Your boyfriend, Dr Hunter, has more intelligence than you, I see!' Petkevich said. 'The first reason I don't kill you now is because we are standing at Aqaba Railway Station. The second reason is that I want you to see me victorious in my mission with the sword! I want you to know how badly you have failed before you die. And I want you to die in the face of God so that you can repent.'

'That clears that up nicely,' Hunter said with a smile.

'So where are we going, Petkevich?' Amy asked. 'Where are you going to kill us all in this grand way?'

'That is not something that concerns you at the moment, Agent Fox. All you need to do right now is keep your mouth shut and do as you are told and then you may live to see a few more hours!'

'That's very nice of you,' Hunter said. 'Always thinking of others.'

Petkevich now ordered his men to come forward and escort Hunter and the rest of the team off the platform and down into a nearby car park. The team climbed into dusty Land Rovers which Hunter thought had been hired to take them out into the desert somewhere near Aqaba, so he was surprised when the journey in the vehicles lasted a matter of minutes before pulling up at a small private airfield just outside the town. Parked up on a large concrete apron were two Russian transport helicopters, with their rotors already whirring. Someone in the vehicle convoy must have radioed ahead and told the pilots to get the engines running while they were driving from Aqaba station out to the airfield. Things were moving fast.

Another crackle of the two-way radios triggered the armed guards in their Land Rover to order them outside into the heat of the day once again, where they were gathered fifty yards or so south of the helicopters while Petkevich and his men in the lead Land Rover stepped out, put on their sun hats and had a short conversation. Then Jophiel walked around to the rear of the lead Land Rover and opened the tailgate before leaning in and pulling out the sword. This was walked to the first transport chopper ahead of the first wave of Petkevich's men, who now followed with the man himself, while Jophiel walked over to Hunter and his team and ordered them into the second transport chopper. Three more men were behind Jophiel.

Jophiel said, 'These men are Tkachuk, Novik and Zhuk. They will ride with you in your chopper and if you disobey them, they are authorised to shoot you through the head. I trust that this is perfectly understandable to all of you.'

'Seems fair to me,' Hunter said.

They climbed into the second helicopter and as they buckled up, Amy turned to Hunter.

'Just where the hell are we going that requires a helicopter, Max? I think it's time you spilled the beans and told me what you were going to say back on the train.'

'The fact we're in Aqaba is a clue,' Hunter said. 'But with that clue alone I couldn't be sure because there are several relevant locations in this area within range of these helicopters. But there is another clue. When Petkevich spoke the prophecy, he referred to a flame of fire.'

'So where is he taking us then?' Jodie asked, butting into the conversation.

Raising his voice to be heard over the sound of the rotors as the pilot increased the power ready for take-off, Hunter leaned closer to Amy and Jodie, who were now sitting opposite him in the helicopter. 'I think we're going to St Catherine's Monastery, right at the south of the Sinai Peninsula. Today it's a Greek Orthodox monastery, still very much in use.'

Amy and Jodie exchanged a blank look. Neither of them had heard of the location, Hunter could tell by their faces.

'What is that place, why is it in the middle of the desert and why would we be going there?' Amy asked all three questions at once.

'It's a very ancient monastery,' Hunter began, 'located at the foot of Mount Sinai itself and built around one and a half thousand years ago. It's actually the world's oldest continually used monastery within the Christian religion, and was built after the Byzantine emperor Justinian the First ordered it to be constructed around the location where Moses saw the Burning Bush, also referred to in the Second Book of Moses as the "flame of fire".'

'The Burning Bush?' Jodie asked. 'I heard something about that. It's another Bible thing, isn't it?'

Hunter refrained from rolling his eyes, recalling Jodie's difficult formative years and her lack of formal education.

'The Burning Bush,' he began, 'is a story in the Old Testament of the Bible, specifically in the Book of Exodus, about when Moses witnessed a bush that was on fire but was never burnt up entirely by the flames. The Bible claims that the Burning Bush was located at the exact site where God told Moses to lead the Israelites into Canaan from Egypt. As you can imagine, it is a very sacred site within both the Jewish and Christian religions and many believe even to this day that it is the location of considerable divine powers.'

'Why would Petkevich have a different prophecy to me?' Toussaint asked, bewildered. 'The Guild and the League guarded the same prophecy for millennia!'

'But you guarded it in different ways,' Hunter said. 'The Guild only ever spoke of it and never wrote it down, but the League kept written records until the time of the monk Uladzimir. I hate to be the bearer of bad news, but I think you're the victim of a kind of Chinese whispers but across many centuries. I think over time, the Guild's tradition of handing the prophecy down only by the spoken word meant that subtle changes occurred.'

Toussaint's crestfallen face tipped down towards the floor and he shook his head, muttering to himself in French. Hunter understood how he must feel, but his thoughts were broken by the sound of Amy's voice, once again bringing everyone back into focus.

'Why exactly would Petkevich want to go there?' she asked.

Hunter shrugged. 'If the Bible tells us that the Angel of the Lord appeared in the Burning Bush and gave Moses his instructions, it may be that its location really is a source of divine power, and I guess that Petkevich believes this very strongly if he is taking the Sword of the Archangel Michael to the location of the Burning Bush. Maybe he believes bringing these two divine powers, one from the Old Testament and the other from Revelation in the New Testament, will create some kind of incredible force unexplainable by modern science.'

'But the monastery authorities surely won't allow that to happen?' Amy said.

'No, I would imagine they would not be up for letting that happen,' Hunter said. 'Which is why Petkevich has remembered to pack twenty mercenaries, all armed with machine guns.'

'Oh, my God! You can't be serious!' Amy looked horrified. 'We can't let Petkevich massacre all the people working at the monastery!'

'We can't let Petkevich massacre us, either,' Hunter said. 'I'm still a young man with hopes and dreams.'

Amy gave him a look and did not restrain herself from rolling her eyes. 'You can be such an idiot sometimes, Max. You know what I mean.'

'And you know what I mean too,' Hunter said, suddenly growing more serious. 'Of course we're not going to let them just kill everybody at the monastery!'

Amy looked into his eyes. 'So you have some kind of a plan then? Because the way I see it, we're heavily outmanned and outgunned.'

'Of course I have a plan,' Hunter said. 'I just haven't thought of it yet.'

## 31

Hunter gazed out of the window as their helicopter came in to land just south of the monastery. The complex itself was an enormous construction including a main monastery building and dozens of other smaller support buildings all surrounded by a colossal fifty-foot stone wall. The massive size of the ancient complex, however, was dwarfed by the size of Willow Peak behind it, considered by religious authorities as being Mount Horeb from the Bible.

Hunter was aware of the site because it was a UNESCO World Heritage Site, first recorded in a journal written by a female pilgrim named Egeria, who described the site in Latin at some point in the 380s AD. The building he was currently looking down on was built nearly two centuries later in the 500s, having been constructed on the orders of Emperor Justinian, as he had explained earlier to Amy. Despite his employment by UNESCO, Hunter had never had cause to come to the monastery and was excited to be able to visit it, despite the circumstances.

Ever since its construction way back in the time of Justinian, it had been visited by people across the centuries. The monastery's influence and business increased after the time of the First Crusade, and buildings were added to it throughout its existence, including even converting one of the chapels to a mosque during the Fatimid Caliphate in the tenth century. More recently, the increasingly radical Islamification of the Middle East caused Islamic State to attack a checkpoint in the proximity of the monastery where they killed a police officer and injured three others in 2017.

But Hunter's primary interest in the site was its library, which he knew thanks to his UNESCO involvement, was the oldest continuously open and operating library in the world. It contained the largest collection of manuscripts and codices anywhere on Earth outside of the Vatican Library. For such a place to exist in the middle of rocky, mountainous and desert terrain was a marvel to a man like Hunter, and despite the horrible circumstances, he was hoping that there would be time for him to visit the library if he could deal with Petkevich and his sinister plans before they caused any damage to the site.

Damage to a location like this would be unforgivable, not simply because of the buildings themselves but also because the site contained the largest collection of religious icons and art from the Crusades anywhere on Earth, a collection which was practically priceless due to its rarity and expansive size.

The helicopter set down just outside the monastery's southern perimeter, and moments later Hunter and his team were ordered off by Tkachuk and other armed guards. Hunter stepped out under the whirring rotors of the chopper and while being beaten by their downwash, stared out across the flat, rocky landscape to the vast monastery a few hundred yards away. To the building's west was a large collection of pencil pines, yew trees and Cypress trees, in a small stone-walled garden, but aside from this, the entire view could almost have been on Mars. It was an amazing achievement that such a wonderful monastery had been constructed in a place such as this, but Hunter's captivation by the view was rapidly ended when Zhuk struck him in the back with the butt of his machine pistol and ordered him forward.

Hunter turned, bristling with rage and feeling a strong desire to punch the man in the face when he caught Amy's eye. She gave a subtle shake of her head, which was enough to calm him down and make him turn back and continue his journey down the path to the monastery. Quinn and the other original party of hostages were being led down to the monastery behind them. He saw Novik had dropped back to guard them and was training a Makarov pistol on Quinn. Behind them, Jophiel was carrying Blanco's backpack, presumably once again concealing the sword.

'What do you expect to achieve here today?' Hunter said to Petkevich.

'I don't believe that's your concern, Dr Hunter,' Petkevich said. 'Just keep walking down to the monastery and mind your own business. You will see in good time.'

'But it is my own business, Petkevich,' Hunter said, unable to conceal the contempt he felt for the gangster a few steps ahead of him. 'I'm a doctor of archaeology and I work for UNESCO.'

'And I am a professor of archaeology who also works at UNESCO,' Juliette Bonnaire said from behind. 'So Dr Hunter is right when he says it is our business. In fact, it is more our business than yours, Monsieur Petkevich.'

Hunter wondered how Petkevich would react, considering Juliette may have angered him with her tone, but instead, he merely laughed and turned to speak to them while continuing to walk, now backwards. 'Then perhaps it is your business too! But as you will both be dead within the hour, I fail to see what relevance this has.'

Hunter was not concerned. He'd heard many threats like

this from men like Petkevich over his years working with the HARPA team and was certain he and his fellow teammates could find a way to overcome Petkevich's force and save the monastery.

'What do you hope to do with the Sword of the Archangel Michael here today?' Amy asked.

'As I just said to your colleague, you will see in good time, Agent Fox... and not before.'

Petkevich turned and continued his passage down to the monastery.

'How the hell did he get permission for these helicopters to land?' Amy asked. 'I mean, there are checkpoints here for cars. There is an authority here that must approve tourists to visit.'

'I don't understand either,' Hunter said. 'He's obviously had permission from the authorities to land. He must have lied about his intentions here today.'

Blanco shuffled forward to join them. 'This place is pretty amazing, don't you think?'

'You can say that again,' Hunter said. 'I just love sites like this. It's why I spend so much of my life out in the desert, looking at ancient sites. In places like this, I feel most like Indiana Jones. Damn it! I wish I had my hat.'

Amy rolled her eyes. 'Never mind your hat, Max. What about your plan?'

'I'm still working on that,' Hunter said. 'I think it might have to be one of those "play by ear" plans where we see what unfolds in the monastery itself, rather than create something clever out here without knowing what's going to happen.'

Amy shook her head, but Blanco was on board. 'There's no way we can know what's going to happen inside that monastery. I mean, look at the size of the place! It's like a small town out in the middle of the desert, all completely encased by this massive stone wall like a fortress! There's absolutely no way we can know what they're going to do. Max is right.'

'But I think I know what Petkevich is going to try to do,' Hunter said, keeping his voice low. 'I was explaining to Amy on the helicopter, Sal. This is the location where Moses saw the Burning Bush and where God told him to lead the Israelites out of Egypt. If you take any of the Bible literally at all, this is going to be one of the most powerful sites of God's power on Earth across the entire world. I think that our host wants to join the power of the Archangel Michael's Sword with the location of the Burning Bush.'

'And then what?' Blanco asked. 'Just see what happens?'

Hunter shrugged. He really did wish he had his hat – the Sinai sun was beating down on his neck and he could really feel the heat. He was thankful the shade of the monastery was only another minute or two away.

'I have no idea what he expects to happen,' Hunter said. 'I'm an archaeologist, not a religious historian. My knowledge of theology has only built up in my mind over the years from various excursions I've made to the world of archaeology. I'm aware of the story of Moses and the Burning Bush, and thanks to my employment at UNESCO, I'm aware that this monastery was built around that site to protect it. As for what happens if you place the Sword of the Archangel Michael on that exact location, you're asking the wrong guy.'

Petkevich now led the team into the shade of the enormous stone wall and walked up to the main entrance, which was unguarded. They stepped through a shaded, arched tunnel to the other side of the thick stone wall where they were met by an elderly man in full archbishop's regalia and his small coterie of smiling officials.

Petkevich stepped forward. 'I trust everything is in order, Archbishop?'

'It is indeed,' the old man said. 'I have all of your papers from the Ministry of Tourism and Antiquities, and everything seems to be in order.'

Petkevich turned and gave Hunter a greasy smile. 'Dr Hunter, allow me to introduce the Hegumen of the Holy Monastery of God-Trodden Sinai, Archbishop Atticus Diakos of Sinai, Fara and Raitho Damianos, as I believe is his full title. Archbishop, this is Dr Maximillian Hunter, an archaeologist working at UNESCO, and his superior, Professor Juliette Bonnaire.'

Hunter glanced at Novik in the other group, still pushing the Makarov into the small of Quinn's back, and knew the part he was expected to play to keep her alive.

'Good afternoon, Archbishop.'

Juliette played along, too. '*Bonjour.*'

'Welcome to you all,' Diakos said warmly. 'Please, won't you come in. I must say, Mr Petkevich, I was very grateful when your office telephoned me and told us about your extremely kind donation to the monastery. I can tell you this is the single largest gift we have ever received in our long history. It was most generous.'

'It was a privilege for me to make such a donation, Archbishop,' Petkevich said smoothly. 'And it is an even greater privilege to have been received here today personally by yourself and allowed such unfettered access to the entire monastery.'

'You are very welcome, Mr Petkevich. Later, after you have looked around freely, I would very much like to have a small meeting in my office in which I can detail some of the very wonderful things we will now be able to afford thanks to your donation. There are several repairs and much construction work to be done here at the site and many other charitable good works that we will be able to contribute to thanks to your generosity.'

'Think nothing of it,' Petkevich said, exchanging a quick look with Zhuk and Novik, who were just behind him. They returned his stare and then carried on walking into the heart of the monastery.

'Tell me,' Archbishop Diakos said. 'Is there anywhere in particular you would like me to show you? Perhaps I could have one of my best tour guides take you around the entire monastery so you're able to get a fuller picture of what we have here. A finer appreciation, so to speak.'

'No, that would be quite all right, thank you, Archbishop. We would like to walk around by ourselves and take in the entire site in our own time. It's so very beautiful here and I'm aware of the general location of everything as I greatly researched this wonderful site before making my donation.'

'Of course you did,' Diakos said. 'Then please excuse me as I have much business to attend to. When you are finished looking around, please go to the main reception area here at the monastery and they will direct you to my private office.'

'Thank you, Archbishop. I will do just that.'

Hunter watched Archbishop Diakos strolling off down one of the many shady, stone-walled alleyways inside the monastery and then saw Petkevich turn swiftly to his men.

'Right. You know what to do, so let's get moving.'

## 32

The inside of the monastery had surprised even Hunter with its complex labyrinthine nature. It was, as Blanco had earlier observed, more like a small town than a mere religious site. Everywhere he looked he saw sandy-coloured stone walls, alleyways, nooks and crannies, and if he looked up, he was able to see the domed roof of a chapel here or a church tower there. Even the familiar outline of a mosque was visible from his position.

They gathered beneath a raised wooden walkway in the shade, surrounded by citrus trees and yucca plants which added a welcome dash of green to the otherwise sandy, dry ochres of the monastery's interior. Hunter read this landscape as a double-edged sword – it could be the kind of place where they could disappear in a hurry if they had to, but it was also the kind of place they could get split up and lost in if things got out of hand with Petkevich and his Illuminati soldiers. He didn't have further time to think about what was going on before Novik walked over to him with the Makarov in his suit pocket, obviously pointing at him through the fabric.

'You're coming with me,' he said. 'All of you. And don't think of trying anything stupid, because my colleague is standing right behind you.'

Hunter glanced over his shoulder and saw Tkachuk standing at the back, also holding a Makarov in his pocket. He didn't think it would take too much for either of these men, or Jophiel or Zhuk, who had gone ahead with Petkevich, to pull these guns out of their pockets and fire them openly in the monastery. He was also not forgetting the half dozen men back in the transport chopper armed with compact machine pistols. They were there for a reason, which right now he hoped was merely backup.

'Why? Are we going somewhere nice?' Hunter asked. 'Are you going to buy us lunch?'

'Just get moving,' Novik said.

Hunter followed the direction Novik had gestured and stepped briskly down a cool, shaded stone alleyway around the monastery until arriving at the location the monastery authorities claimed was the original Burning Bush as seen by Moses over two thousand years ago. Petkevich and his two bodyguards were standing right in front of it. Zhuk now opened up Blanco's backpack and pulled out the sword while Novik stood guard at the end of the other alleyway which approached the Burning Bush from the opposite direction, ensuring no one could get through. Tkachuk now took up a position behind the group, stopping tourists or monastery workers from approaching from the direction they had just come from.

Zhuk now handed Petkevich the sword, causing Simeon to gasp in horror at the events unfolding right before him. Toussaint made the sign of the cross for the third time since Hunter had met him, lowered his head and began mumbling a prayer in French.

Petkevich began reciting the Bible as he took hold of the sword and walked it over to the Burning Bush.

'"Now Moses kept the flock of Jethro, his father-in-law, the priest of Midian: and he led the flock to the backside of the desert and came to the mountain of God, even to Horeb. And the angel of the Lord appeared unto him in a flame of fire out of the midst of a bush: and he looked, and, behold, the bush burned with fire, and the bush was not consumed. And Moses said, 'I will now turn aside, and see this great sight, why the bush is not burnt.' And when the Lord saw that he turned aside to see, God called unto him out of the midst of the bush, and said, 'Moses, Moses.' And he said, 'Here am I...'"'

'Just what the hell's going to happen now?' Jodie asked.

'Please, Jodie,' Amy said. 'Language.'

Hunter felt like smiling at Amy's admonishment of Jodie's inappropriate language but was suddenly frozen in place by the sight of the sword in Petkevich's hand as it began to glow. At the same time, the Burning Bush above Petkevich also started to glow, at first a dim orange colour almost impossible to see, as if it were being lit by a setting sun, but then it gradually grew brighter.

'I don't think I like this very much,' Blanco said from behind Hunter.

'Me neither,' said Quinn. 'I wish I was very far away from this place.'

'Is not good,' Volkov said.

'Everybody, just take it easy,' Jim Gates said. He was still comforting his wife with an arm around her shoulder, but naturally took the leadership position over the HARPA team. 'Just everybody, take it easy. We don't know what's going to happen. It could be in our favour after all because Petkevich is one evil bastard.'

Juliette Bonnaire was standing with her hands on her cheeks and her mouth open in total mystified silence, while Volkov began shaking his head from side to side, almost unable to believe what his own eyes were telling him.

'Really is not funny,' he said.

Petkevich walked the sword closer to the Burning Bush, raising its point until it almost touched it. Hunter now watched the sword growing in brightness, so brilliant that it was lighting Petkevich's face almost as if he were holding a mirror that was reflecting the sun's light up onto him. It was changing from orange to white, as was the Burning Bush, and Hunter was aware of heat emanating from the bush as well as light. In the background somewhere, he didn't know from where, was a low humming sound.

'What's that noise?' Amy asked.

'I don't know.' Hunter looked around to try to find the source but saw nothing that hadn't been there five minutes before. The peace of the desert was slowly being encroached upon by the strange humming which now gradually seemed to be turning into a rumble, accompanied by a low, almost undiscernible vibration they could feel through their feet.

'Max, now I'm scared,' Amy said.

'You're scared?' Hunter said. 'You went to Sunday School in Boston! I have only been to church for weddings and funerals. I'm not ready for Judgement Day!'

'Is not funny either,' Volkov said again.

Hunter knew it wasn't funny too, especially as Petkevich began to tremble and gradually shake where he stood.

'Throw the sword down!' Jophiel said. 'You cannot control power like this!'

'I can't!' Petkevich said, his voice thick with panic. 'I can't throw it down. It is stuck to my hands like a magnet!'

The shaking became much more violent. Hunter thought that it was going to tear the Belarusian's arms right off his body, and now his head was going up and down violently and wildly from side to side, his eyes rolling up into their sockets and his tongue lolling out of his mouth. The glow had now become a piercing bright, blinding light emanating simultaneously from the sword and the Burning Bush, and bolts of a strange, thin type of electricity began leaping between the two ancient religious objects. Slowly, Petkevich was dragged closer to the Burning Bush. It seemed to Hunter to be sucking the sword towards it.

Archbishop Diakos and several of his officials ran into view, easily able to get past where Novik was supposed to be guarding because the Illuminati man had turned to stare dumbly at what was happening to Petkevich. Hunter watched, dumbstruck, not even knowing what to think as the archbishop and his officials scrambled closer to Petkevich, clearly not knowing what to do or even what they were seeing. The archbishop pulled himself up fast and made the sign of the cross before raising his hands to heaven and beginning to pray in Greek. His officials swarmed around, trying to control the terror of the tourists. No one knew what was happening.

There was now a blinding flash that knocked everyone's vision out for a few seconds. When Hunter was finally able to see again, Petkevich was on the floor beside the sword, stone-cold dead with his face frozen in a rictus of terror. Jophiel, Novik, Zhuk and Tkachuk were stunned, not knowing what to do for several seconds. Then Zhuk opened fire on HARPA and screamed at the others in Belarusian.

Hunter pushed Amy out of the way to avoid her taking a bullet and felt a searing agony as the round tore through the deltoid muscle of his upper arm. He grunted in pain as the hot lead shredded the soft tissue and missed his humerus bone by half an inch. It felt like someone had punched him harder than he had ever been struck before.

'Are you okay?' Amy cried out as the two of them crashed into the alley wall a few yards away from the Burning Bush.

Back up against the wall and breathing heavily in the hot, dusty air, Hunter ripped the hole in his shirt a little bigger and examined the wound. 'Another few mils and it would have hit the brachial artery, so I guess that means yes, I'm okay.'

'Thank God,' Amy said, with a glance up the alley to the Burning Bush.

'The bleeding is moderate,' Hunter said as he tore off his shirt. 'I have an idea.'

'Really, Dr Hunter,' Amy said, her eyes flashing over his chest. 'I salute your optimism but this is neither the time nor the place.'

Hunter gave her a look. 'I make the jokes around here.'

'Do you? I hadn't noticed.'

Now, he smiled and handed the fabric to Amy. 'Here, you can stem the bleeding with this.'

By the time Amy had tied the makeshift bandage, everyone else had scrambled for whatever cover they could find. The ground was still shaking beneath their feet, and the roaring noise somewhere in the distance was receding but still rumbling away. Chaos now exploded over the entire monastery; as Zhuk darted forward to grab the sword, Archbishop Diakos ran towards him and pushed him back, but Zhuk fired a bullet into him and then reached for the sword. The wounded archbishop cried out in pain, lunged at him, summoning all his strength to push him over, and then he hefted the sword, pointing it at Zhuk, who took one look at it and disappeared down the alleyway behind the Burning Bush.

Jophiel had vanished. Novik and Tkachuk fired into the crowd, aimlessly killing two or three tourists. Hunter knew the intention was to sow panic and terror across the entire complex before trying to make their escape. Novik now fumbled in his pocket for his radio, which he snatched out and lifted to his mouth. He spoke in rapid Belarusian, and Hunter didn't need to know a single word in the language to understand he was calling the choppers and preparing them for an immediate escape.

Hunter turned to Amy and the others. 'Me, Jodie and Volkov are going to go after those bastards! Amy, I think you should stay here with the others and look after the archbishop. Someone needs to make a phone call and get some kind of a medical helicopter out here. This is an emergency!'

Hunter sprinted away down the alleyway, with Volkov and Jodie right behind him. There was only one thing on his mind and that was ending this nightmare for good.

## 33

Hunter ran down the dry, hot alleyway in pursuit of Zhuk, Novik and Tkachuk. The way they had taken had been the fastest escape route away from the chaos back at the Burning Bush, but it was also running in the wrong direction from the helicopters. Hunter knew their priority would be to change direction and get around to their left before turning and running back down through the monastery towards the entrance they had used on their way in. They had failed in their mission and their leader was dead, for all they knew, struck down by God himself. All these men wanted to do was flee with their lives. Hunter wasn't going to let that happen. He wasn't about to let men like this live to fight another day.

Hunter ran blindly up the alleyway before being forced to turn left at a bend where he was confronted by the site of Tkachuk standing at the far end of a new alley with his gun raised into the aim. The Belarusian fired, and the bullet hit the wall behind Hunter's head and ricocheted off into the blue Egyptian sky. Hunter was lucky the shot had been high because he hadn't even had time to try to avoid the bullet by ducking.

Tkachuk didn't hang around to improve his aim with a second shot and now darted out of sight to the right.

'Hurry up!' Hunter called out to the others. 'We can't let them get back to the helicopters.'

'At least those bastards haven't got the sword any more,' Jodie said.

'Who would want it?' Volkov said as they ran down the alley. 'After what we saw back at Burning Bush, I certainly would never want to touch such a thing.'

They reached the end of the alley and Hunter peered cautiously around the wall but saw no sign of Zhuk and the others.

'They must have gone down here because there's nowhere else to go,' Hunter said.

'This place is like a damned maze!' Jodie said.

Off to the left, they all heard gunshots and screaming. Hunter calculated that from the sound of the screams and shots, the Belarusians must have turned and were now making their way towards the entrance. 'C'mon! This way!'

The team ran past one of the chapels and then down some steps, running down another broader pathway shaded from the hot sun by olive trees and citrus trees. When they reached the end they could see the monastery's main entrance. They were just in time to catch sight of the Belarusians as they ran through the entrance, pausing to shoot some of the security guards who had tried to stop them from leaving the compound. In the background, Hunter heard the sound of the helicopter rotors powering up ready to airlift them away.

'We haven't got much time left!' Volkov said.

'Run faster!' Jodie said.

Hunter sprinted down the last of the steps and ran over to the dying security guard. The man spoke very poor English, and

Hunter didn't know what to say to him, but when the security guard reached for his gun and handed it to him, Hunter understood that language perfectly well.

Hunter checked the gun's magazine was loaded and then the three of them sprinted out of the monastery. The Belarusians were halfway up the hill on their way towards the transport choppers. Hunter saw Jophiel in the lead, almost at the helicopters.

'Bad news,' Hunter said. 'The men armed with machine pistols are coming out of the choppers and taking up defensive positions around the undercarriages! They're opening fire!'

Hunter and the team dived for the cover of the low wall running around the outside of the main monastery compound and returned fire, instantly taking out Tkachuk, who was running at the back. He now smashed into the ground and tumbled over and over in the dust before coming to a rest at the side of the path in some gravel. He was lying flat on his back, his dead eyes staring up at the sky. Up ahead, Jophiel was climbing inside a helicopter.

Volkov managed to take out two of the men with machine pistols. Tkachuk's death had caused enough of a stir among the Belarusians to order an immediate retreat. The men with machine pistols now followed Novik and Zhuk into the helicopter and Hunter watched Zhuk slam the side door shut. It looked like the pilot of the first helicopter was talking to them over the radio – Hunter could just see him with his helmet and visor down speaking into his mouthpiece as both helicopters began to lift off the ground.

'What are we going to do?' Jodie asked.

'There's only one thing left to do!' Hunter now broke cover and sprinted up the path towards the helicopters, each one now more than twenty feet high and rotating, ready to fly away over the mountains. Volkov was right behind him, and Jodie was a few yards behind him. The three of them fanned out, with Hunter taking the lead helicopter with Jophiel on the left and Volkov and Jodie running to the right and attacking the helicopter with Novik and Zhuk on board.

Hunter fired at the windscreen of the helicopter, emptying his magazine and praying to whatever God had just killed Petkevich that his aim was true. He received the answer to his prayers when his bullets punched a line of holes in the windscreen and took out the pilot, but was then confronted by the horrifying spectacle of the enormous Russian transport helicopter falling out of the sky directly in his direction.

It was a nightmare made real as Hunter ran for his life off to the left, the sun flashing on the hull of the chopper seconds before it ploughed into the ground just yards away from him. It detonated and exploded into an enormous fireball, the shock-wave blasting Hunter from his feet and spewing an enormous mushroom cloud of black smoke up into the air. Hunter was sent rolling in the dirt and gravel and dust before finally coming to a stop, coughing and spluttering. He had lost his gun somewhere in the fall, but it was of no matter because he had emptied the magazine on the pilot.

He looked up, wiping the dust out of his eyes just in time to see Volkov and Jodie repeating what he had just done, with Volkov aiming at the pilot and Jodie aiming at the fuel tank. The two were competing to see who could bring down the helicopter first, but they were being hindered by the men with machine pistols who had now opened the side door and were returning fire.

Hunter was terrified for Jodie because she was on exposed ground, well outside of the monastery, and had no cover. He now watched hopelessly as his friend and colleague was chased across the mountainside, with machine-gun bullets tearing into the ground just inches from her heels. She dived for the somewhat inadequate cover of a small boulder, but what really saved her was the angle of the mountains in front of her, which caused the helicopter pilot to break away and bank hard to the right.

This was a stroke of luck because now Volkov had a clear shot at the pilot and he opened fire in the same way Hunter had done, punching holes in the windscreen and killing him instantly. This time the helicopter was flying towards the monastery, and Hunter held his breath as it roared out of the sky towards the ground, certain it was going to smash into the ancient building and cause irreparable damage and endless headlines around the world. Luckily for everyone, it came down to the ground two hundred yards short of the monastery and exploded in another enormous fireball, repeating what he had seen moments earlier and spewing up a massive, filthy black cloud of smoke and gravel and bent metal and human body parts in a giant explosive cloud of horror.

But it was over. Hunter collapsed back down into the gravel, staring up at the sky, and almost felt like laughing. Still on his back looking up into the blue, he called out, 'You okay, Jodie?'

'Yeah, I'm okay,' she said. 'Assholes nearly got me though.'

'What about you, Volkov?' Hunter said. 'That shooting was nearly as good as mine.'

'Is not true!' Volkov shouted back.

Hunter smiled and finally got himself up on his elbows just in time to see Jodie and Volkov walking over to him. He crawled up to his knees and got to his feet and met them halfway. For a few seconds, the three of them just looked at each other in silence, then Hunter surveyed the two burning wrecks on either side of them. Up above, the blue sky was gradually turning black, and the smell of burning aviation fuel turned his stomach. Inside the monastery, he could still hear the screams.

'Hey, you hear that?' Jodie asked.

'You mean the screams?' Hunter asked.

'No,' Jodie said. 'The rumbling that started after Petkevich tried to touch the Burning Bush with the sword. It's stopped!'

Hunter cocked his head and focused carefully. Jodie was right. He could no longer hear the roaring and rumbling. There was no more vibration, no more shaking of the earth. He didn't know what to say so he said nothing. Then the three of them turned and walked slowly back to the monastery.

They were greeted inside by the applause of the surviving security guards and the archbishop's officials, who quickly shepherded them back around to the Burning Bush where the archbishop was now up against the wall. His breathing seemed to be a little easier and Susanna Gates had dressed his bullet wound with a tourniquet and some sterile gauze pads from first-aid supplies in the monastery.

'Is he going to be all right?' Hunter asked.

As he spoke, Susanna Gates was still fussing around with the archbishop, trying to make him more comfortable. Jim Gates nodded at Hunter's question. 'Susie says he's going to be fine. It was just a flesh wound.'

'Thank God for that,' Jodie said. Everybody turned to look at what she had just said, and then the gravity of her words seemed to strike her. 'Well... I think in this case that's really what happened, don't you?'

Hunter turned his eyes from Susanna Gates helping the archbishop and shook Jim Gates's hand. 'It's good to have you back, Jim.'

'It's good to be back,' Jim Gates said.

'You can say that again,' Juliette Bonnaire said, leaning forward and kissing Hunter on the cheek. '*Merci bien*, Max. I mean that, from my heart.'

Hunter looked at Quinn, the last member of the four rescued

hostages. She was leaning up against the wall in the shade of an olive tree and seemed to be extremely unimpressed by everything that was going on around her. He wandered over and asked her if she was okay.

'Yeah, I'm good. Thanks for what you did.'

'We all did it,' Hunter said. 'We pulled together just like we have so many times in the past. Only this time it was the most important mission of all – saving our friends.'

'I'm not sure that was the important part,' Quinn said. As she spoke she was looking across at the sword, which had been positioned carefully beside the archbishop.

Hunter squeezed her shoulder and then walked back over to the others. His first stop was Mentor Toussaint and Simeon.

'How are you two holding up?'

'We're okay, thank you,' Toussaint said.

'We are better than okay,' Simeon said. 'We have spoken to the monastery's officials and they have agreed to let us stay here to help look after the sword!'

Hunter hadn't considered where the sword would be going next, but this made about as much sense as anything else he could think of. There were few places on Earth with this much religious significance and which were this remote. If they couldn't hide it away somewhere safe here, then no one could. He was also pleased to hear that Professor Toussaint, Simeon and the rest of the Guild of St Michael had found a new home.

'Well, I wish you both well, gentlemen,' he said. 'And thank you both very much for risking your lives to save my friends.'

'And the sword,' Simeon said with a smile.

Hunter shook both their hands and walked back to the Burning Bush. He couldn't take his eyes off the sword the entire time and was half wondering if its proximity to the Burning Bush would set off whatever had happened before. Now his eyes turned to Petkevich's corpse, which someone at the monastery had covered with a white sheet.

'Exactly what happened here today?' Hunter asked no one in particular.

Archbishop Diakos spoke, softly but clearly. 'The wrong man asked the wrong question of God. That is what happened here today.'

Hunter and Amy's eyes met, and with the archbishop's words still hanging in the hot, dry air of the very same courtyard that contained Moses's Burning Bush, Hunter knew it was time to go home.

## 34

Blanco felt the heat from his brother Angelo's old brick pizza oven as he walked past it on his way through the kitchen. He was still getting used to using it because it took a lot more skill to use than a regular oven, but it gave the pizzas a wonderful wood-fired, smoky flavour underneath the delicious toppings that Blanco's was so famous for. Rocco, the head chef who ran the restaurant, was using a pizza shovel to pull out one of his latest creations, and Blanco just caught a glimpse of the beautiful margarita pizza as he brushed past him.

'Fantastic work, Rocco!'

'Thanks, Sal. I saw that Florentine pizza you made yesterday, and I think maybe I got some competition!'

Blanco thanked him with a pat on the back and carried on his way. His new world of dough mixers and industrial refrigerators, mozzarella cheese, the smell of warm yeast or freshly cut vegetables and the shining chrome of pizza cutters was a far cry from anything he had been used to in the army or working with the HARPA team. But it was a good world and a world he was pleased to be part of. His brother Angelo had opened up a second Blanco's restaurant, expanding the franchise, and had hired him to work there. Rocco was the head chef because he had a quarter of a century of experience in the pizza restaurant business, but Blanco was co-owner of the restaurant with his brother. It was a good arrangement, and his brother told him that once he had more experience with the business and the creation of the pizzas, he would be able to buy a third restaurant which Blanco could run. That was just fine with him. Blanco liked things slow, easy and predictable.

And Blanco liked learning things, the latest being Rocco's tutorial on how to create beautiful high-hydration dough. He had shown him how to give the dough a long and very cold fermentation in one of the fridges to produce a pleasing flavour and superior texture.

Blanco now walked to the next oven and used a shovel to extract his own creation, handmade by himself just a few minutes ago. It looked great and he was secretly proud of it. He slid the pizza onto a serving plate and walked it through the kitchen, through the double doors and out into the busy restaurant. It was a great location, and every time he stepped out of the kitchen and looked through the large window running all the way around the outside of the restaurant, he was given a beautiful panoramic view of southern Manhattan. Now he walked the pizza over to the best table in the house and set it down in between Quinn Mosley and Jodie Priest.

'Man, that looks good enough to eat,' Jodie said.

'I hope so,' Blanco said. 'You guys mind if I join you?'

'Are you kidding?' Quinn said. 'That's why we came to this place. Oh yeah, and I heard the pizzas are really good too.'

'I hope so, but you gotta be honest,' Blanco said. 'This is one of the first ones Rocco let me make entirely on my own. I made it just for you guys because I didn't want to serve it to any real customers.'

Jodie laughed but Quinn was already tucking in, leaning forward and pulling a slice of the freshly baked pizza off the plate and onto her smaller dinner plate. With a gentle pinching of the crust to stop the tip from sagging, she now raised it to her mouth and took a bite of the delicious, freshly baked bread and topping.

'Oh, man that is fantastic,' she said.

Blanco looked eagerly at her, his eyes wide with anticipation. 'You really mean it?'

Quinn now had too much in her mouth to reply to Blanco's question, so she instinctively covered her mouth with her hands while she chewed and nodded her head, also managing an okay sign with her left hand.

Jodie also helped herself to a slice and took a bite. She had opted for a more modest bite, allowing her to deliver the verdict more clearly. 'Best pizza I ever had, Sal. You think you could open a restaurant in California?'

Blanco felt a surge of sadness spoiling the moment. He sat down beside Jodie and looked at her, feeling like a father whose daughter had just told him she was moving out to live with her boyfriend. 'You're going to California?'

'At least temporarily,' she said. 'Since HARPA was suspended, there's nothing for me in DC any more and I don't know anyone in New York.'

'You know me.'

He recognised the emotion behind the look she just gave him – he was a father figure to her but not somebody she could centre her life on. He understood. She wanted to strike out on her own and start a new life somewhere. She was brave enough to do that, but she wanted to do it where she grew up.

'I'm going to miss you, Jode.'

'Listen, we can Zoom, right? You can visit whenever you want. And when I want one of these pizzas I'm going to come straight back here to New York.'

Blanco laughed along with her, but with the extra decades of experience he had on his side he knew they were unlikely to see each other much more, despite what she thought. That just wasn't the way things worked out when people said goodbye to one another and made solemn promises to catch up, especially if they were heading to different ends of a large country like the United States. Blanco had a strange feeling that unless the HARPA team was pulled back together by Jim Gates, he would probably never see either Jodie Priest, Quinn Mosley or Max Hunter or even Amy Fox ever again. But that's what life was about, he thought. In life you spend time with people, you get close to people, and for those brief fleeting moments, you thought they would last forever but you never saw the true transient nature until the moment was over and everyone went their separate ways.

'Okay, that sounds just great to me,' he said. 'We'll make sure we keep up with one another whatever we do. What about you, Quinn?'

Quinn made a gesture, raising her arm, flattening her hand and pointing it down towards the ground. 'I'm going underground. Down into the shadows, into the hinterlands of the cyberland.'

'Seriously though?' Blanco asked.

'Yeah, seriously,' she said, taking another slice of the delicious pizza. 'I'm going to disappear again. That's what I do best. I'll go someplace I've never been before and just disappear inside a computer. It's what I am.'

Blanco looked at the young goth, trying to conceal the sadness he felt for her. He'd known her for many years, but like everyone else on the team, he didn't really truly know her. She had come out of nowhere and now she was going to go back to nowhere, disappearing into the shadows like a wraith. What she did there, he could only guess, but he knew it would involve computers, the internet, and hacking. She would get paid large sums of money by rich people with poor computer skills to do things they wanted to do but couldn't do themselves. He didn't want to ask too many questions. He wanted a simple life, a life he understood, and that meant making pizzas and drinking wine and going for walks on sunny days in New York City.

The three old friends finished the rest of Blanco's first pizza, chatting about the rest of the team. They had heard through Amy that Jim and Susanna Gates were planning to move house, away from the place they had been kidnapped from by Petkevich's men, and set up a new home somewhere in an unknown location. That didn't surprise Sal Blanco – Jim Gates was the kind of man who got in touch with you, but you didn't get in touch with him.

'Here's to ending Oriax,' Blanco said, raising a glass. 'Or Petkevich, if you prefer.'

The others joined the toast. 'To ending Oriax.'

'For as long as I do this job,' Jodie said, 'I'll never understand what drives people like that.'

'In his case, a sense of rage and betrayal,' Quinn said.

Blanco and Jodie turned to her, both with a similar expression of intrigue on their faces.

'You did your thing on him?' Blanco asked with a smirk. 'You dug up the dirt! You gotta tell us what you know.'

'Yeah, fess up, sister,' Jodie said.

Quinn gave a typically nonchalant one-shoulder shrug. 'It was easy enough – just a few minutes at a keyboard.'

Blanco leaned in. 'And what did you find?'

'Aleksey Nikolayevich Petkevich, born in Minsk in 1971 to a

poor farming family. He followed one of his uncles into the Eastern Orthodox Church and became a priest, but after developing radical solutions to what he saw as a world of sin, he was defrocked.'

Blanco smiled. 'If Hunter were here, there'd be a joke coming along right about now.'

'Which is one of the many reasons we can all be grateful he is not here,' Jodie said with a twinkle in her eye.

'Defrocking,' Quinn continued, 'is also referred to as laicisation and involves formally stripping priests of their clerical rank and removing all their authority. Petkevich responded to this worse than most, you might say, and vowed revenge not only on his former church but the entire world.'

'A measured and sane reaction,' Jodie said. 'Not.'

'Either way, he's no harm to the world now,' Blanco said. 'I say we forget about it as best we can and move on with our lives.'

'Amen to that,' Jodie said.

At the end of the pizza and the wine, Blanco wanted to keep talking. He knew what would happen when he stopped talking but he had to let nature take its course, so with the last sip of wine in his glass he raised a toast to the HARPA team and then to the three of them. They chinked their glasses and drank the wine and then made their goodbyes. Walking to the door, the three of them stepped out onto the busy Brooklyn sidewalk, and the city's lights sparkled to life around them as they made their final goodbyes.

'Have a safe flight to California, Jodie,' Blanco said.

'I will.'

They hugged for a long time and then broke apart, pausing for a moment to grip each other's hands.

'You too, Quinn,' Blanco said. 'Wherever it is you end up, I hope things work out for you. Have a safe life.'

The young goth stood on tiptoes and kissed Blanco on the cheek and then stepped away.

'I will,' Quinn said.

She turned and walked north before disappearing into the subway station. Then Jodie said goodbye to Blanco one last time and turned and walked south, turning the corner of the next street and disappearing out of sight.

Blanco stood alone for a few minutes on the sidewalk, with a white baking cloth over his shoulder that he'd forgotten was there and had been there through his entire meal. He looked out across the lights of Manhattan and wondered where all the years had gone. Jodie and Quinn had their whole lives ahead of them, years of unexpected adventures, twists and turns that couldn't be anticipated, and he knew in their hearts they both enjoyed a sense of eternal life that all young people lived by.

Blanco on the other hand knew how quickly those years would go by, but he had no regrets. He'd worked as a soldier in the US Army, he'd flown helicopters for them, and most recently he had travelled the world with the HARPA team and seen things that the men and women he saw moving past him now on the sidewalk could not even imagine. Just a few short days ago he had been in the oldest continuing working monastery on Earth, and the very same location where Moses had witnessed the Burning Bush, where God had spoken directly to him. Experiences like that were as rare as a white fly, as his Italian mother used to say.

But now it was time to settle down to the most important mission of them all.

Making the perfect pizza.

## 35

'What's the problem?' Hunter asked Amy.

'Nothing,' she said, clearly meaning 'something'. 'I was just expecting something a little different, that's all.'

'Like what?'

They were standing on the modest balcony of Amy's George-town apartment. Now, she shrugged, sipped some beer to buy some time and smiled. 'I don't know – maybe some spicy jerk chicken, or barbecued pork ribs. Cajun-spiced chicken skewers? And some barbecue sauce. There isn't any barbecue sauce.'

'That's because this is a British barbecue and not an Amer-ican barbecue,' he said smugly. 'A British barbecue is a very different animal from an American barbecue. The American barbecue is comprised of a vast range of tastes and flavours and spices, most of which have been shamelessly poached from Mexico. The British barbecue, on the other hand, is a much more subtle and modest affair. The British barbecue is very often simply some sausages and maybe a salad comprising of some lettuce, tomato and cucumber. Anything more than that might be considered an extravagance. And when I say sausages, I mean proper British bangers, not what you mean by the word sausage, which is some bizarre patty thing or something I've never been quite sure about.'

He looked at Amy, who was keeping her counsel and trying hard not to smile.

'Perhaps,' he continued, 'if we're feeling extremely extravagant we may cook some beef burgers as well. And maybe if it's a very special occasion there may be some fried onions. What you are looking at here is a classic British barbecue. You will of course forgive us for not having developed the art to a more complex level than this, but that is primarily because the British climate only offers enough days of sunshine for perhaps half a dozen barbecues every year, and that is on a good year.'

Amy was still completely silent, now sipping some more beer and sliding her sunglasses over her eyes. She was clearly enjoying Hunter's verbose lecture on the subject of Alfresco dining.

'If,' he went on, 'it stops raining for long enough to barbecue outdoors, this is how we will enjoy ourselves. Some sausages, some burgers, and a nice modest, basic salad. This is why you will not find any caramelised, barbecued, Cajun-spiced smoky beef brisket or deep-fried green beans covered in a large quantity of rich creamy dressing while I am holding the tongs.'

Amy could contain herself no longer. She burst out laughing and then said, 'I think your barbecue looks absolutely fantastic, Max.'

'No, you don't.'

'I do, I really do!' Amy said, not sounding in any way convincing. Now she lifted her sunglasses again to get a clearer look at the sizzling meat down on the hot plate. 'Tell me, is it normal in British cookery for the sausages and burgers to be black like that?'

'Black like what?'

'Um, rather well done.'

Hunter paused and turned to face her, pointing the barbecue tongs in her face. 'They are not rather well done. They are nicely caramelised.'

'They look like they're made out of charcoal.'

Hunter looked down at the sorry selection of meat he was cooking for their lunch and found it hard to argue otherwise. 'Yes, I will perhaps concede that they are slightly overdone, but I'm sure the interiors are perfectly fine. Here, pay attention.'

Hunter now deftly utilised the tongs to pull a sausage from the hot plate and set it down on a white china dinner plate beside the barbecue. Holding the sausage with the tongs in his left hand, he now pulled a steak knife from the side and cut the sausage open to reveal an almost totally raw interior.

He frowned. 'Hmm.'

Amy finished her beer, looked at the bloody sausage and then up at him. 'Is that how they like them in Britain, too?'

'All right,' Hunter said. 'Even I can't explain this. We can't eat this so what the hell are we going to do?'

'You wanna go out to a restaurant or get a takeout?'

'That question poses a significant dilemma,' Hunter said, also finishing his beer.

'No, it doesn't. I think we should get some pizza delivered to the house.'

Hunter shrugged and set down the tongs. He poured a pitcher of water over the hot coals, putting the barbecue out of its misery. 'Yeah, I can go along with that. It's a shame we can't get one of Sal's pizzas. I'm dying to try one of those.'

'Well, unfortunately, it's an hour and a half's flight to New York City, plus all the time you have to waste at the airport each end. I think for now we're going to have to make do with the delivery from the local restaurant.'

'Sounds good to me,' Hunter said. He leaned over into the ice bucket where they had some cold white wine chilling and poured them each a glass. It was an Australian pinot grigio, something he had read about in a magazine a few weeks ago and had ordered specifically through a local wine merchant.

Amy took her first sip and sighed with satisfaction. 'This wine is beautiful.'

'It certainly is,' Hunter said. 'I'd say not as beautiful as you, but it's a bit on the nose.'

'And very cheesy,' Amy said. 'I'm glad you didn't say it, but you kind of did say it.'

Amy's phone rang. She checked the caller ID, but Hunter didn't have to ask to know who it was. She answered it immediately.

'Ben? How's your son?'

Hunter couldn't hear Lewis's reply, beyond some low mumbling sounds on the other end of the line. Amy went inside and paced the room. For a second, Hunter believed Lewis's son had died, then Amy stepped back outside and breathed out a long sigh of relief.

'Thank God for that, Ben. I can't say how happy I am to hear he's going to be okay. You must be so relieved. How's Meg?'

More mumbles, then Amy said goodbye and turned to Hunter. 'You heard the good news?'

He nodded. 'I did. Thank God.'

'They stabilised him a couple of hours ago. They think he's going to be fine.'

'Good old Ben. Anything to get out of a mission.'

Amy gave Hunter a look. 'I'll call the rest of the team and let them all know.'

Amy went back into her apartment. Hunter watched the clouds scudding over the sky for a few minutes and then Amy returned, having given the good news to everyone else. She was beaming. Hunter gave her a kiss and then the two of them stepped in from the balcony and moved into her living room. Amy picked up her phone to call the local pizza restaurant as Hunter crashed down onto her long leather couch and sighed with relief. He sipped more of the wine, set the glass down on the table beside the couch and closed his eyes for a moment, recalling what he had seen back in Sinai.

In all of his long years' experience as an army officer out in the remote desert sands of Afghanistan and Iraq, and all of his years working as an archaeologist for UNESCO, not to mention the various missions he had successfully completed with the HARPA team, Hunter could never really remember a time he felt such fear and awe as he had felt back in the monastery when that rumbling and roaring started just after the Burning Bush began to glow. He didn't know what any of it meant, but he knew it wasn't his place to be asking questions about such an extraordinary event. He understood people through history had claimed to have witnessed God or his works, and he wondered if that was what had happened to them back in Egypt so recently. Of course, it was all idle speculation as Hunter knew only too well, having seen many odd and curious things in his time that raised questions in his mind. He had learned to file most of these things away and not let them bother him, but something told him what he had seen in the Sinai would not be forgotten quite so easily. He wondered if Amy and the rest of the team felt the same way he did about it, but couldn't see any reason why they would not. In this regard, the small group of friends shared something personal that very few other people in the world would ever appreciate.

When Amy had finished ordering the pizzas, he opened his eyes and looked at her.

'What do you think happened back there?' He didn't need to specify any more than that.

'I think maybe it's how the archbishop said it was, that Petkevich was an evil man and he tried to use God to further that evil.'

'But something happened though, didn't it?' Hunter said, perhaps doubting his own memory. 'I mean, I didn't imagine what happened to Petkevich when he held that sword and the bush began to glow, did I?'

Amy shook her head and reclined in her chair. 'No, you didn't imagine it. And we didn't imagine the rumbling and the roaring either. But I don't know what it was, Max. Maybe it was just some scientific thing. Some earthquake thing, some kind of crazy coincidence.'

'You can't really believe that.'

She shrugged. 'Or maybe it was what the archbishop said. I don't know and I'm not sure I want to know. We've come a long way since we discovered Atlantis together and I've enjoyed everything we've ever done, but it has raised some serious questions in my mind. What happened back in the monastery is probably the most serious of them all. And I don't know how to answer it.'

Hunter didn't know how to answer it either. The two of them spoke about the monastery, and their other missions – the discovery of Atlantis, the Revelation Relic, the incredible moment they saw the bow section of the *Titanic* raised from the Atlantic floor, and then their hunt for what they had believed was the sword of Excalibur but what had turned out to be the flaming Sword of the Archangel Michael. It was an incredible whirlwind tour of history both hidden and recorded.

No matter how hard he tried, he couldn't imagine what could possibly top these adventures, and the recent communication from Jim Gates to Amy explaining HARPA had been suspended, pending a full investigation into their latest mission, suggested to him that he would not get the opportunity to try. Was he sad that the team had been temporarily suspended? He wasn't sure how he felt about it. Juliette had offered him a full-time position back working for UNESCO, but he wanted to spend more time with Amy, not less, and Amy's family and work opportunities were to be found right here in the Washington DC area.

He couldn't expect her to move away from her entire life so whatever he was going to do, it would have to be here in DC or around the city. He supposed he would end up at Georgetown University teaching archaeology, and he certainly would have no problem getting some pretty amazing references to help secure whatever position he wanted. It was easy for him to imagine himself settling down with Amy somewhere around here, and there were far worse lives to lead, as he knew only too well from his time in the army. Would the HARPA team ever be recommissioned and would he ever be sent back out into the field with the best friends he had ever known? Only time would tell. He wasn't even sure if that was what he wanted out of life any more. Could anything really beat the breathtaking spectacle of witnessing the Burning Bush coming to life again after so many thousands of years? Perhaps it was time he settled down to an ordinary life, an ordinary commute, and teaching a new generation of students about the amazing wonders of the classical world.

He and Amy wandered back out to the balcony and spoke for a long time. He had always enjoyed her company and the more he spoke to her, the more he noticed her brilliant mind and a sharp and entertaining sense of humour that always kept him on his toes. He did not know when it had happened, but at some point in the last few years, he had realised that he didn't want to spend a day without the company of Amy Fox. He knew she felt the same way about him because she had said so in their quieter moments together. Now, they watched the sun move down towards the western horizon, and sparkle on the waters of the Potomac down at the end of First Street.

'Like I said,' Amy said after a while. 'I just don't know how to answer it.'

The doorbell rang.

'But I know how to answer that,' Hunter said. 'I'll grab the pizza and pay the guy, you top these glasses up with some of that beautiful wine. We might not have the answer to every question in the universe, but we've got each other and we've got tonight.'

Their eyes met and they touched their two wine glasses together.

They were home.

\* \* \*

## MORE FROM ROB JONES

The next book in The Hunter Files series from Rob Jones, *The Vatican Conspiracy*, is available to order now here:

https://mybook.to/VaticanConspiracy

# AUTHOR'S NOTE

It was tremendous fun bringing the Hunter team back together again – I always really enjoy writing all of my series, and The Hunter Files is no exception thanks mostly to Max, Amy, Sal, Jodie and Quinn, who are always good company. I hope you enjoyed it too, and stay tuned for more Hunter Files!

# ABOUT THE AUTHOR

**Rob Jones** has published over forty books in the genres of action-adventure, action-thriller and crime. Many of his chart-topping titles have enjoyed number-one rankings and his Joe Hawke and Jed Mason series have been international bestsellers. Originally from England, today he lives in Australia with his wife and children.

Download your exclusive bonus content from Rob Jones here:

Follow Rob on social media here:

facebook.com/RobJonesNovels
x.com/AuthorRobJones

# ALSO BY ROB JONES

**The Hunter Files**
The Atlantis Covenant
The Revelation Relic
The Titanic Legacy
The Excalibur Code
The Angel Prophecy
The Vatican Conspiracy

# Boldwood

Boldwood Books is an award-winning fiction
publishing company seeking out the best
stories from around the world.

**Find out more at www.boldwoodbooks.com**

Join our reader community for brilliant books,
competitions and offers!

Follow us
@BoldwoodBooks
@TheBoldBookClub

**Sign up to our weekly
deals newsletter**

https://bit.ly/BoldwoodBNewsletter